where is this place that i feel at home, where
where is th[illegible] place that i feel safe and secure
where is th[illegible] place that belongs to me, where
my prom[illegible] land [illegible] me, [illegible] Jerusalem
where is [illegible] t[illegible]at [illegible] ry my heart
Where oh where oh where do i belong

home

home

Home / hōm / noun: the place where you live, where you belong, where you are safe and secure to be yourself, to live your dreams

Published by Hallard Press
Papakura
Aotearoa/New Zealand
2013

ISBN 978-0-9876529-8-0
(c) David Gadd

Home is one of a series of collected short stories. Some of the stories within this series have appeared in other collections or publications. Others are published for the first time. This is the first time all have been brought together in one collection.
Home is also available as a Kindle ebook.

Cover and inside design Hallard Press.
Cover photography - Stock footage provided by yellowj / Pond5.com
The person depicted is a model and their likeness is being used for illustrative purposes only.
Inside and back cover photography - Hallard Press

CONTENTS

love cannot blunt
the huge strangeness of us
each the totem post
deep impressed of forebears alien

TOKERAU

This is the simplest sort of a story, it's not really a story at all, it's just about me.

I was born up North, way in the sticks. The old lady's house where we lived was up on top of a steep bluff, bracken and scrub all down the long slope of it to the road. On the other side of the house was the little plot of ground. My mother gardened, you know - pumpkins, corn, potatoes, beans (runners up their wire-netting, the broad beans and the French beans in straight rows below), peas, some berry bushes, some citrus fruit trees. She kept us well supplied, and that was good because it was quite a drive to the village down the road. The land just behind Mum's little cultivated squares looked overgrown with scrub. But in £act there was enough clear land for Dad to run beef cattle as well as our own milk cow.

From the front porch of the house you could look over and down and see a kilometre or two away a line of tall trees. That was where the marae was, our family's, with my uncle's old broken-down house right alongside it. Not a flash marae, nothing like the carved places you see in pictures. No, just a square, flat-roofed dining hall, and the flagpole, and the wharenui itself exactly like a church hall, with its name written across the door's lintel and no other decoration outside at all. We are a plain people, I suppose, we northerners, us Ngapuhi, down to our earth. My aunty used to tell people, strangers, that this was because the Ngapuhi were more concerned in the older days with arts of war than with those of peace. But it's not that at all. My grandfather would say it, "this is where New Zealand begins." What show could say more?

The house site, my mother's house, was so elevated you could see an uninterrupted view on every side. No other rise of land could match that of our little plateau. We looked out upon a rolling landscape of farms and pockets of bush, and slopes of scrub, a green green, a wide, beautiful prospect. We could follow the sun its whole day from rise to set, nothing able to shadow our house. Even from the earliest years I could not imagine myself leaving this place forever, but could visualise myself one day, as my mother had done, bringing home someone with whom to share this house, this entire place.

The urgings by my grandfather (he lived in Kaikohe) to acquire a good education, to stick to school until I graduated with as high a qualification as it was in me to get, are among my earliest memories. "Look at us," he was fond of saying - sometimes you had the impression that he used his family to tryout phrases for his oratory - "the people of the Tail of the Fish. The Pakeha have been with us since the days of Captain Cook, and we are still here. No, no, in spite of what you sometimes hear it is not the pressures of the Pakeha ways of life that can do us harm. It is failure of the spirit which is the root of those harms that fall upon our people."

A good thing about our family was that no one - not even my mother with her often blunt and straight-from-the-shoulder comments nor my grandfather - tried to lay down for me what I had to do with my life. And yet by the time I was coming to the age of needing to think towards high school, I knew it was true, that I did want to stay on at school, acquit myself well, qualify myself. I wasn't sure how this could be done, however - my mother didn't ever stop reminding me that we were poor, that education wasn't cheap.

My father seldom had much to say. One day while I was milking the cow, he came down and stood at my shoulder. He said, "Tokerau, girl, what is it you want? Do you want to stay here with us and travel to high school each day on the bus? Or do you want to go away to a boarding school? It's your choice."

"I want the best kind of a high school I can go to Dad," I explained to him.

"Then you'd better go down to Auckland." And I did, with the help of the Maori Education Foundation. I was accredited U.E. at that city school.

My wanting to return to my home never faltered. In fact our high school teachers inspired us with ideals of using our knowledge to serve our people. They made my will all the stronger to go back up North, home.

The tough choice of those school years was to find a career to let me do that. I thought of the post office. But I couldn't see that a vacancy at the single proper post-office in the entire district would come up for years. Nursing? But like working in the Bank and similar jobs, it meant living in the largest township of our part of the North, far, far, far from home. There was only one job that seemed to fit my wishes. Schools were scattered up and down the Fish's Tail, every scale, so to speak, with its own little school. Some were closing, but so many remained. I trained for primary teaching. In my first year I managed to get a post at a school not far out of Auckland so that I could do some University courses in the Maori Studies Department.

My father had an accident, he could not work. He and my mother, they insisted that I go back to my classroom to wait in the city until a position closer to home offered.

The waiting was years. Good years, though. There was so much to do, so many people to know, so much newness to adapt to. The secretest part of me that knew its home never changed.

My parents passed away, within months of each other. And so, shocked, I knew their house, their land, was my responsibility. As I emerged from the car, I could feel I was here for good, for good. My husband looked around, looked down uneasily, almost dizzily. That first day I found myself leading him by the hand, showing him what refreshed me, soothed, reassured, gathered me into itself. Nothing he could attempt could stop his boredom thrusting at me. In the end, my husband spoke to me frankly. He could not live the life that had bred me. No, it wasn't that our love was deficient nor that our differences could estrange us. It was simpler, that the world of each of us failed to nourish sufficiently the loved one. He travelled back to the city. Our life with each other has become an intermittent thing, we holiday as it were with the other, live the most of the year apart.

Now I want to tell what drove him to his city, what is my daily grief yet somehow makes me cling the firmer here.

This landscape I look out over morning, midday, evening looks so much the same as when I was a child, a green farmscape. There is more scrub, I think, than before. But behind our house the land is taking on a different appearance for a whole huge quarter of the View. Our own land, you see, is rented out to the forestry company whose rows of young pines stretch out into the distance. In the other direction, along the metalled road, is a line of great, grey stumps rotting where the line of trees once had protected the marae. On the overgrown paddock no buildings stand, fire gutted years back they were not replaced. For the people have left. They are in the towns, the city.

It is a landscape of emptiness. What need have trees of people? My school dreams of serving my people are as mocking as shadows.

I stay. My love for all this that I see has not altered, I shall stay. I keep from me thoughts that one day our people may return. Who can foretell, who dares?

I'm not lonely. There's the telephone, the TV, the country roads to the little town where our people collect occasionally to a hui. There is the road I take a few times a year to the city. There are neighbours, distant Pakeha neighbours, as friendly as when I was younger.

I told you this wasn't a story. It all leads up to nothing. Just to me gazing out upon this whole landscape from which I will not, I cannot move away. Its changes hour on hour, season on season rhythm in the pulses of this flesh, glow to the days of my looking. It is Tokerau.

WHERE TO GO?

The rest of the kids had run howling to other parts of the house. And Mum, she was really getting stuck into me. My own tears I couldn't hold back because she'd got me on the cheekbone just where there was a bruise still. I couldn't get away from her, she was holding me so tight - and she's bigger than me!

It was all over nothing. Yes, I'd got home late again. OK, but my mates, their parents don't care too much when they come in. Yet Mum and Dad are really old fashioned - they want to be as strict as back home in the islands. They really try to hammer their ideas into me. Look, I know they mean well. I don't want to worry them or even, you know, defy them. But they don't see my point of view, ever. I mean, like sometimes you've really got to go with your friends, eh. And you just can't always get home when you said. But it's all a new kind of life to them - still after all these years. And they simply don't get how different it is, how utterly, utterly different it is from back home - well, I can't remember it, but to them it's always home. If I try to talk with them, explain my thoughts, they tell me, 'We won't talk about it - you do what you're told, no argument.' And if I ask them to explain their ideas to me, they say, 'Too many questions. You answer your parents back?'

I think at these times I see in their faces a fear I am growing away from them, turning into someone they can't understand. And maybe they fear I'm just the first - it will happen again and again as each of their other kids in turn grows up. What can I do?

'You wait till your father gets home, girl, he'll make you learn,' my mother told me in our language (her English goes out the door when she's angry), her words coming out in jerks between her fists hitting me. That did it! I could not - would not - take any more of this.

She was getting tired. I could rip my jersey from her hands. I raced out of the house mopping my eyes with my sleeve as I went like a little kid. I was getting surely too old for this sort of thing.

My mind was clocking over fast as I ran. I wasn't going back in there in a hurry. I'd go to my married cousin. She'd put me up. I'd stay there a while. I'd share a room with her kids, or anyway there was a settee. And anyway their place was nearer the high school than ours was. Good.

Clothes I'd have to borrow until I could persuade my cousin to go home and pick up things for me. And my school bag and books. But me, I wasn't going back, not for a good while. No one was going to thrash me around again. I stopped sniffling and I hurried along the concrete footpath. Things would be all right, I could feel it.

Well, my cousin didn't argue too much. Matter of fact she didn't even seem all that surprised to see me, either. She gave me a bed and put her two littlest children to sleep together in one bed in the same room as me. They didn't mind. They liked having me in the room with them. And I didn't mind too much sharing with them - it was better than going home! I think my cousin was happy, actually, to have me around the place. (I wasn't going out till the worst of the swelling had gone down - and I could stop holding my neck as if I was trying to poke it through the side of my collar. I even took a couple of days off school.) She liked going to housie and stuff sometimes at nights. So everything settled down smoothly.

Her husband said when he came home and found me still there after a couple of days, 'You, you're old enough to get a job.' He sounded just like Dad telling me exactly the same thing. 'Shut up, you,' my cousin was quite angry with him. 'Mind your own business. She has a good education to get, like we never had.' But he glared at me. 'And I'm supposed to keep her too am I? Pay for all the food she eats, the electricity from watching the telly, what about some rent then - I can't support freeloaders.' But my cousin just told him to shut it again and he went off grumbling to himself into the kitchen to fix himself a feed. They had a funny sort of life, she and this husband of hers.

He was her second husband. I used to like her first husband really well. This guy, well he had a little moustache and long sideboards and gingery hair and thought he was really neat. He was on the night shift. So he'd be around the place when I came home from school and go off to work in the evening then come back in the early hours of the morning before anyone was awake. He was always having a dig at me, on about money or food. That seemed to be all he cared about. I know my cousin was cool with me here, was really supportive, but I heard him and her have a niggle about me every now and then and it didn't feel good, me bringing this disturbance into their life. But she kept saying it was OK, so I tried to forget it and get on with things.

My cousin told Mum and Dad everything when she went to get the clothes and so I decided I'd wait till they got in touch with me. But they didn't ring or come round or get in touch. So I could be proud too. It hurt - and I guess they were hurting also - but that's how I felt. I was still pretty wild with them, see. But otherwise things were quite good. My cousin's a hard case, good fun to be around.

Until one morning. Some sound must've woken me. It was light all right, but I could tell it was still very early. The kids were both sprawled out asleep. And there was my cousin's husband. My eyes nearly slipped out of their bones with surprise. He was looking real ugly at me. And he had a knife in his hand, even in that room with curtains drawn that knife managed to pick up a finger of light and it gave off a real mean gleam. 'I'm home from work, I've got a hunger and what do I find - I went to the fridge to get a slice of that cold roast girl, and it's gone. All gone, girl. ' He started coming towards me. I didn't wait to find out what he wanted - I could guess it didn't involve talking about this calmly. And thing is, I didn't even eat his stinking meat, but that was no time to try diplomatic negotiations. I just bolted out of bed. I flung the window wide and scrambled out over the ledge, my legs and arms still weak from sleep and shock and scraping on the brick. I must've made a bit of noise because I heard my cousin call out to know what was going on. I crouched on the grass behind a bush. I heard the kids whimper a moment then a door close. I peeped through the window. He'd gone from the room. I climbed in quickly and with hands that kept shaking pulled on my clothes over my night things. I pushed all my stuff I could see into my school bag. One of the kids opened a big brown eye and I whispered to him to go to sleep. I could hear arguing in the next room. I sneaked through the house and out the back door. And took off down the road. I just couldn't stay there. No matter what my cousin said, staying there just wasn't going to end well.

Home - I stopped in my tracks. All the old bruises suddenly seemed to ache again. Oh no, not that, not that. Their love for me was just too drastic. I couldn't bear that again just now.

Sleepiness or something seemed to get in the way of my thoughts. I couldn't decide what to do. Where to go? All kinds of people - friends, relatives, even teachers - jumbled through my brain. I thought I heard a voice calling. I looked up. And there was a car sitting on the grass by the road. I could see the keys in the ignition. I went up to it and noticed that the passenger's window was not wound up. A door slammed loudly somewhere close. Suddenly it was like someone else was sitting in my mind. I threw my things on the back seat and slid across to the driver's seat, put on the seat belt (I'm very law-abiding really, my parents have rubbed that into me!) and started the engine. Even while deep inside me I was telling myself, Hey, don't do this! But the things my boy friend of last year showed me came back to steer my hands and feet. The engine roared a bit. I didn't want to wake up the car's owner. So I let out the clutch and was off driving slowly, getting more confident. Now I could go where I should've gone first time - to old Aunty Seilala. Now I had wheels I could get there no sweat. Look, there was even plenty of gas.

She would let me stay. I could talk with her, and she'd talk to Mum and Dad, they'd sure have to listen to her. Right away I was very happy. Everything was at last going to come right. Maybe I could shift in with her till I finish school!

I had a sudden thought. I hoped the owner of this car was still snoring so he couldn't miss it and give the number to the police. I kept an eye wide open for cops. And I had to whip quickly around a corner one time to avoid a cop car. But at last I arrived at Aunty's place. It must have been about seven o'clock. Damn, I'd left my watch.

What to do with the car? I parked it round the corner from Aunty's place, just like in TV. I felt bad now about taking the car. But, well ...

I came through her door hugging my bag and shouting out (she never locks the door no matter how many times we all tell her), 'Guess who's here?' No sound. I remembered that the people who'd been keeping an eye on her had been sent back as over-stayers. Perhaps her niece who lived here had had to go on night shift too. I shouted out again. Must be really sound asleep.

I dumped my stuff on a chair and went into her bedroom.

She wasn't asleep. My heart thumped like a clenched fist in my chest. She was half in half out of the bed, gasping, her face a terrible dark colour. She sort of mumbled something at me in our language and I couldn't make it out. I bent down to her and tried to heave her back on the bed. 'Hey, I go for a doctor,' I told her. Her eyes crinkled up as they did when she was puzzled. Maybe she was too sick to remember her English. I said it in our language. She made a pointing with her hand and I saw on a stool a piece of paper with a doctor's name and address printed on the top. I raced out and telephoned that number. The phone was engaged. I could hear her breathing even out here.

I was too scared to panic. I shouted out, 'I'm going to the doctor.' I would have to leave her alone again. I ran fast as I could back to the car. I wasn't exactly sure where the doctor's place was, but thought I knew near enough. I roared the car round in a circle up on to the footpath and down again and down the road, and around the corner, the tyres screeching.

And that's when you got me. And that's all there is to tell.

And I sure hope while you've had me waiting round and making me talk and all, you've had someone to get that doctor and someone to fetch one of her family to be with Aunty Seilala.

OK, OK. So I'll go home with you now. (But do we have to go in that police car?) And you'll go off thinking you've done a good day's work sorting me out. And my father will maybe thump me again. And then we'll all cry over each other, and explain how much in spite of everything we love one another. And in another week's time something - anything - will happen and we'll be back to fighting again and I'll be maybe running off to - well, someone's place.

Because, you know, even parents and kids can live in worlds so different. My parents' minds and hearts will forever be back across the ocean. Back in places I can't remember. While I've grown up to a teenager in this city, this is my world. I can't live by ways I don't understand and I don't even know about except for the bits my parents tell me every now and then. You see, not even love can squeeze out all the differences and make us like - like, well all right, like a tapa cloth, joined all to a single sheet.

All I want is a place for me - a place just to be me. Is that too much to ask? I guess it is, eh.

Well, come on then, take me back, police lady, and let's get the bad parts over with.

TO JERUSALEM

'Jerusalem, it's way way down a big river,' said Pati.

'I know that place,' said Hoani, 'there's some holy people there. They look after children and people. We used to sing a song about that: 'He said bring the children to me/Even far across the sea."

'I've seen pictures of it,' said Pati. 'There's soldiers with guns to protect everybody. Ba-a-a-a-bam!'

'And there's that big river, and it's always sunny there, and there's houses with funny roofs and deserts and trees and there's all kinds of things there.'

'They've got a big temple too,' Pati said.

'My sister said there was a big big river down somewhere close here,' said Hoani.

'I don't know what's its name.'

'That's the one, maybe, eh? Could be. It's somewhere down the line from here, I think so.'

'Everyone seems to like it, you know, that Jerusalem.'

'Might be we could go and have a look one day.'

'Eh! Why not? There's nothing to do here.'

'Well, come on.'

When they got to it, they stared at the motorway. 'You're not allowed to walk down there,' said Pati.

'Who says?'

'My big brother. You can get hurt. Or maybe the police will catch you.'

'Not true,' said Hoani. 'I've seen what you do. You do this, see? That's hitch-hiking. People give you rides in their cars.'

But it was a long time, hours and hours, before any car stopped. It was a man in a little old car. 'What are you kids doing?' he asked them.

'We're hitchhiking, see.'

'Where?'

'We're going to Jerusalem,' said Pati.

'That place on the big river down from here,' said Hoani.

'Yes? I think I might be able to guess where you mean,' said the man doubtfully. 'What about your parents. Do they know what you're doing, where you're going?'

'Oh yes, they know Jerusalem,' said Hoani. 'They're working today. We have to go by ourselves.'

'Seems a funny business to me, two kids on their own hitching like this,' said the man.
'Will you take us there, please?' said Pati.
'Hm,' the man hesitated, looking at them. 'I think I've figured out where you're talking about. Well, OK, hop in, I'll see you get there. But I sure hope I'm doing the right thing. Don't know what some parents are thinking of.' He glanced at their bare feet to see how dirty they were.
It was a very long way to Jerusalem. It was fun in the little car as they raced down the motorway, sometimes even passing big cars and lorries. Then they got off the motorway and into a lot of traffic. But in a little while they were driving through the countryside. Soon it was not so interesting. It was all the same things to see all the time. Sometimes they passed through a small village. The man did not say much to them. He was frowning a little bit. They got sleepy with all the driving. And he gave them lollies to keep them awake. Then he said, 'Look, here's the river.' They drove over a wide, green river on a huge bridge. Boy, it was high. And the river was so big you couldn't see where it started or where it ended. Across the bridge the man stopped the car.
'Now look,' he said, 'I've come right out of my way to take you here. But I guess you know where you are now. See, there's the first houses just over the paddocks there. But you stick to the side of the road, do you hear, and walk on this side. All right?'
'Thank you,' said Pati. 'You are kind to us.'
'We can walk now,' agreed Hoani. 'Thank you, man.'
'Have a good holiday,' said the man and he drove off.
'Must be Jerusalem,' said Hoani.
'Could be,' said Pati. 'There is the big river, and look - there's some hills, and trees. Yes, and that brown field over there, that's a desert.'
'Maybe we'll see the soldiers soon,' said Hoani.
They were tired of walking along the dusty road by the time they got to the first house. They felt very hungry.
It was a little, old house by itself. Then there was a group of houses, a space, and then they could see across the gardens and some high bushes more houses. But some of them looked like they were empty.
'Well,' said Hoani, 'I guess it is maybe an old town.'
An old lady came out of the house and looked surprised to see them standing staring over her white fence. 'Hullo boys,' she called out.
'Is this Jerusalem?' said Hoani.

'I suppose you could call it that in a way,' she said.

The lady looked just like his Aunty Hana. She smiled. 'You boys are looking tired and hungry to me. Why don't you come in and tell me who you are looking for while I fix you something to eat?'

So while she gave them a feed, they told her how they had come such a long long way from the big city to find Jerusalem, and how they had heard what a good place it was and how the people there liked to have children visit them.

'But what about your parents? Where are they?'

'Oh, they are at work,' Pati explained. 'They have to go early and come home when it is towards dark.'

'They are all working?' she asked.

'All of them,' said Hoani. 'We play by ourselves or sometimes with our mates, and our sisters give us our meal at night before Mum and Dad come home. And our mothers give us some money to get us what we want to eat during the day time.'

'We will go home and tell them about Jerusalem,' said Pati.

For some reason the lady looked a little bit sad. 'Well,' she said, 'you have come a journey all right.'

'Are there some soldiers here?' asked Hoani.

'Soldiers?'

'Yes, to look after the people.'

She smiled. 'Well, I think I can show you a kind of soldier. Come on.'

They walked down the road, past some of the houses, and into a large paddock. There was a place like a church in the middle. 'Look up there, he's our protector, I guess,' said the lady. And right at the top on the front of the roof was a figure of a man in wood with some sort of spear in his hands.

'Is he a soldier?' said Hoani, disappointed.

'Oh yes, he was a real soldier who fought to save his people once upon a time. In lots of battles he was the bravest,' said the lady. Pati was looking hard at the building. It was quite big. It was very dark inside. It had strange markings on the walls and under the roof. It had a bell alongside it. 'Is this the temple?' he said.

The lady thought for a moment. 'I suppose it is a bit like a temple,' she said.

'Can we go inside?'

'Yes, let's do that.' The lady showed them the temple. She told them how it was named for one of the old people of long ago, an ancestor, eh. And they looked up and saw his backbone running all along the ceiling. And they saw his great long ribs stretching down each side of the ceiling towards the ground. And there were paintings on them. And they could see how the whole place was like hugging them in, protecting them. And even though it was dark and strange it felt warm and safe in here with the old lady. And they saw the photos on the walls - and sure enough there were pictures of soldiers in their uniforms.

'Wow,' said Hoani, 'this is a neat place.'

'It is BIG,' said Pati.

They were coming out when an old man called out to the lady. 'What is this, e hoa? Are these some new mokopunaa or maybe some of your own you have been ashamed to show us all these years? Eh, eh?'

'Turituri, hold your talk,' said the lady. 'These are two friends of mine, Pati and Hoani. And they have come from the city to see our place. And they have been wanting to see our house and some soldiers.'

'Soldiers eh?' said the old man, puffing on his pipe. 'I'm an old soldier. Some stories I could tell you about wars.' The boys' eyes widened.

'Don't you go scaring these young things,' said the lady.

'Hush your tongue,' said the old man. 'Do you want to hear some stories, you fullas?'

'Yes, please,' they said.

'Are you a grandfather?' asked Hoani.

'Why, I am a great grandfather,' said the old man. 'Do I look like your grandfather?'

'I have seen my grandfather,' said Pati. 'He came to stay at my brother's place from the islands one time.'

'My grandfather is a very busy man,' said Hoani. 'He lives up north. He is too busy to see us very often. He's very important, you know.'

'Old Eruera here, he will be your grandfather while you are here,' said the old lady. 'And, e hoa, while you tell these boys your stories, I shall go down the road to the Maxwells and telephone the soldiers in blue.'

'What?' the old man stared at her.

Her foot tapped the ground. 'Nga pirihimana (the police), old man, so they can tell these boys' folks where they are and help to take them home.'

'Do we have to go home now?' said Hoani.

'No, no, tomorrow is fine,' said the old man.

'Let it be on your head,' called the lady as they went off. 'I shall come and collect you boys later for your dinner.'

That night they slept together in the same bed on the veranda of the old lady's house. You could see the stars, so many of them, wobbling in the darkness, real close. And a moon as white as a bowl.

They were a long time talking together (quietly in case the old lady heard and growled at them), about the stories the old man had told them. 'Gee, he must've been a brave man! Boy, all those Germans chasing him through that forest!' It was good to talk. It stopped the quietness and there being so few people in the house, being too strange.

It was surely hardly daylight when the old man woke them up. There were two men with him, one of them with a fat stomach. He looked a little bit like Pati's uncle. 'Come on, up, up, up,' said old man Eruera. 'Do you want the eels to get right away?' The two men grinned.

It was very exciting catching those four eels, one of them so long and thick and wriggly. They had to learn all sorts of things so as not to frighten the eels or to get in the way of the men. And they had to help bring the eels up on the river bank. They were really starving when they went back to the old lady's for breakfast. She gave them some of that eel meat, and it was really good.

They were still eating when a few kids arrived to play with them. They went with their new mates and the little brothers and sisters they were looking after to a small beach by the river. (That sand was rough on your feet!) Boy, it was funny, you didn't wear no nothings there when you went to play in the water.

The old lady appeared on the top of the bank with a policeman. 'R-r-r-r-rr.' One of the kids in the water mowed those two down.

'Have the police come to catch us?' said Hoani.

'This is the police of Jerusalem,' Pati told him, 'They don't catch people.'

'Come on you two,' called the old lady. 'Here's Mr Hapi to take you home.'

She had a towel to dry them, and their clothes. They walked up to the road to where the police car was. The old lady cried a little over them. And suddenly the old man was there too to shake their hands. 'When yous come back to see us,' he said, 'don't forget to bring the whole family.'

'Now,' said the policeman, 'if you two jokers haven't eaten too much tucker, you can both sit in the front seat with me.'

The boys and their new mates and the old lady and old Eruera waved and waved as the car drove down the bumpy, dusty road.

'You had a good time here?' said the policeman. (He had a black moustache and when he spoke it puffed up.)

'Yeah, that Jerusalem is a neat place,' said Pati.

'You wait till we tell our families we have been all by ourselves to Jerusalem,' said Hoani.

BACK UP HOME

Six of them, milling around this old guy. Just having their fun. But he looked scared, backed up to the fence, arms up like he thought they'd go for his face. Big kids, few years younger than me, 16 or 18 I guessed. But they were so surprised to see me coming at them, they were hardly ready for me when I moved in, shoving them out of the way. A fist or two grazed my face, someone hacked my shin. I took no notice.

'Cut that,' I said. I glared my eyes round at them, five guys and - look at that - a girl. Not so bad, either.

They weighed me up in their eyes, their fists dropped. The man suddenly shot past me, not so old, that pink bald patch put me wrong. Not a word of thanks.

The kids were wild, they started in to bad-mouth me. They stopped, mouths stuck open. I turned. The guy had crumpled, he was down on the pavement, only a metre or two away. Blood was running from his head.

'Hey, we didn't touch him, just a joke,' one of them said. Then I saw the car head-lights slide down the house wall. A prowl car. And we were like on stage, under the street light. They were going to make a run for it.

'Hold it, freeze,' I said. 'You run and they'll have their fun.' They took no notice, they were taking off, belting down the street.

The car's doors slammed wide. The girl - she'd got a duffle bag over her shoulder - hadn't got so far, stumbled. 'Oh, God!' Her voice was shaking. I moved fast, grabbed her. The cops shouted. I slung her over my shoulder like a sack.

Hid my face. I raced across the road, right in front of a cop. I knew this place. I put my other shoulder to a gate, shot through, slammed, bolted it, tore between the old houses, up a dirt bank, round the factory, into the dark narrow street. I put the girl down. Her eyes glowered at me, she rubbed her ribs where my shoulder bones had tangled with them.

'Hi,' I said. 'Wiremu Hinga.'

'Suzanne.' She was still trying to catch up with her breathing. 'That was one rough trip, man.'

Car lights flashed. I yanked her into a doorway. She was jammed into my side.
'I think he's died,' she said. 'The cops'll think we did it.'
'Right. And they know me, too.'
'Bastards. Some of my mates, the cops know them.'
'Move it,' I said, 'home's along here.'
'Oh come on, you're going to wait for them?'
'No. Just want to get some stuff. This could be bad for me.' She ran, caught up. 'They won't believe me, not with me just off probation.'
'Eh!'
'I'm getting out of here. I know the place to aim for. I'm going up country, back up north, my folks came from there. Time to get out of this dump for a while, anyway.'
'South, that's where my grandmother's family came from, Kawhia way,' she said.
'I haven't been up there in a long time. It's a good place, the best.' I'd been looking her over, real good. 'Come if you want,' I said.

There was no one home. I went into my room. 'Here, take this.' I chucked her the small bag. I was ready. I took up the suitcase and walked out. I heard her coming down the wooden steps behind me.
'Was shifting house, anyway,' she said. 'We walking all the way?'
I didn't feel like talking. It took a while to get to the taxi stand. Expensive, but it got us out of the area quick, up to the main bus depot. And then the long wait for the bus.
The only close family I'd got up in that place in the north any more was Uncle Mack and Hiku. his missus. They were surprised when we walked in, dusty from the dirt road from town. Mack gave us a good welcome. Told us to stay long as we wanted. I told him, 'That bus cleaned us out. But that's a big patch of dirt you've got out there for your garden. We'll give you a hand.'
Mack said, 'You're family, you're welcome. And I won't say no to a couple of extra pairs of hands just now.'
We looked up all the old faces. It was so long, there were plenty of changes, people gone south, people getting hitched, and that. I told those who were thinking of taking off to the city, they were crazy.
'It's OK for you to talk,' said Nathan Te Wao, 'You, stay here if you want to. But nothing much to keep us here, boy.'

But we found plenty for us to do. And Mack took time out to take us fishing in his outboard. Boring - I'd forgotten just sitting there, and early in the morning he went, too. Next time, I left him and Suzanne to it, caught up on some sleep. And he took us way back into bush country, a couple of dogs with us. They bailed up a sow fat as a heifer. We let Suzanne have the killer shot. That was one straight eye she'd got. She was a lot of fun, that girl. (But somehow, all the time, I got the feeling Hiku never really took to her.)

There was one place up there I'd been meaning to look up.

My idea of exactly how a place ought to be.

We walked out there, over the paddocks (no road that far out), down through the scrub where the farmland petered out.

'Oh! Deadly!' She didn't move, only stared. The sun hanging over the sea, the green rollers knocking themselves out on that big curve of beach, sand so white your eyes dazzled, even early as this. The whoosh, hiss of the sea and a gull yokyokking the only noises.

She tugged at my grip. 'I'm going to be the first one to race down that beach. Let-'

We ripped apart. That terrible great noise swooping on us.

She was shivering, scared, crouching on the sand. We stared up.

Nothing.

'Jesus!' she said.

And then there, right above us, you could nearly touch it. A chopper, sliding sideways, tilted, you could see people staring down at us, teeth grinning.

I jumped up, was running, I couldn't keep pace.

A whole big hunk of the bank was ripped up, levelled, only bare clay. Yellow clay and brown dirt spilled across the white sand. The chopper was down, in the paddock beyond. There were guys in the field, holding up poles, guys looking down telescope things. The people were coming down out of the chopper, cameras going, pointing around the place, jabbering.

Suzanne shoved my gear into my hand. I put it on, I couldn't shift my eyes off the place. The pilot jumped down, saw us, grinned, turned away. I charged across the scraped dry clay.

'Hey, you,' a guy was yelling at us, 'stay off this land. This is private property.'

'What the hell you mean? Get off it yourself.'

'Hey, steady on,' he said, backing up. They'd all turned to stare.

'Go on, get off, this is Maori land.'
'Oh no, not one of them!' said a voice.
'Yeah,' I yelled, 'one of them, one of those bloody natives doesn't want you on his bit of land. What the hell you messing here for? Piss off.'
'Now, you just hold it down, you listen to me, young man,' said a tall fulla. The whole bunch of them were coming this way. I felt Suzanne's fingers, cold, dragging on my arm. 'We've explained to you, this is private property, please leave.' Some of them had recognised us by now, I could see their laughing faces. My fists curled.
'You are trespassing.'
'Don't you try that on me, this is Ma-'
'Not so.' The tall guy's voice whipped the air. 'This company has acquired this site from the Crown. You have nothing to do with this land, nothing at all. Leave, both of you, now.'
'Get-'
'Wi, come on, what's the use yelling at them? They'll just get the law.'
'This place, look-'
'Let's split, man.'

'Sure we know about it,' Hiku said when we got home. 'It's the Polynesian Tourist Company.'
'What?'
'They'll fly in wealthy American types right from the airport, up here in their own floatplane. Real high class-'
'Oh, real Polynesian they'll be. Ngati Arizona, Ngati Texas Oil Well. Locals behind the bar only, that what you fullas want out here, Hiku?'
'Sure. It means jobs, money.'
'Jobs? All Pakehas out there.'
'Listen. Roads, buildings, staff-'
'Oh, I get it. Brown road workers, brown bedroom maids laid in a row. And then - of course, I know - the concert parties. "Throw a dollar to the funny brown man sticking out his tongue in the grass skirt, honey - and get yo' lil' blue eyes offa that girl in the topless pewpew-".'
'Don't get sarky with me, boy. That's all right with me. There'll be changes, that's OK. We'll have to take that. But this'll save this community, you thought of that? Look, this sort of thing's going on all over the world. Red Indians and such, they even get in and run this sort of thing themselves. You're out of touch.'

'And we're out of land. And that place, there's hardly anywhere like it left. And they'll have it. That land's rightfully ours.'

'Tell him, Mack,' said Hiku. 'I've got work to do if other people haven't'.

'It's not ours any longer. Been out of our hands just about all my lifetime. Look, there were hardly any of us left up here, even then. This is a tough place to get a living, bring up a family. People were hard up, they didn't know what to do. They worked hard, got nowhere. All they had was land, but no money, no know-how to work it. So it was all over with our land before you were born, I guess.' And he started in on the whole big story.

I told him. 'All this stuff, amalgamation of titles this, crown lease that. Just means they've got our land. And you, you've just got their fencing contract, Sammy Kahu, he has to lease back from them his own land!'

'There was no other way,' said Hiku. 'Get that into your head, boy. We didn't have the legal beagles in those days to help us, we had nothing, just all that dirt and scrub, and hungry kids and whares you city people wouldn't walk into. What's all the interest in it now for, anyway? It was the best could be done.'

'For them, for Pakehas.'

'Don't get your steam up,' said Mack. 'It's all done, that place is going to go up on that bay, don't waste your breath on it.'

'Man, you sure get angry,' said Suzanne when we went outside.

'Where's the point? Nothing you can do.'

'Nothing? Not me.'

'Forget it, it's getting to be a drag. I'm going down to the beach.'

'Yeah. And I tell you what I'm going to do, I'll stuff them right from the start. Tonight, I'm going out to that place, I'll pull out every single survey peg. That should clean the grins off their faces!'

'Bad!' She flashed a grin. 'That's cool! I like that one. I'm with you, turkey. I got a score to settle with those fullas in that chopper too, remember?'

'I'll hitch a ride, too,' said Mack's voice behind us.

'You?'

'Not to help you with those pegs, I'm not getting into that. But I'll be ready for a swim out there, the time I'm finished with those fence posts this afternoon. See you.'

'I like that guy,' said Suzanne. 'He's pretty young to be your uncle, ain't he?'

Turned out, I pulled most of those pegs myself. Suzanne sat down on the sand and said she'd got something in her foot.
'I can fix it,' said Mack. So I left them to it. When I got back Suzanne had two or three of those pegs. I chucked the lot in the sea. Mack was towelling himself down.
"I've got a sweat up,' I said, 'let's have that swim.'
'I pass,' said Mack.
'I'm on,' said Suzanne, 'could do with another one.'
'I've got to hit the sack. Yous both walk home,' Mack said.
I told him, 'You're getting out of condition, you'll be an old man before you know it.'
'Don't you count on it,' said Mack.
'Listen,' I said, later, we'd buried ourselves among the bushes, it was getting cool. 'I might stay on up here a while. Might even find a job. There's Sophie's place up the road a bit, I can use it if I want, it's empty now. You gonna stick with me?'
'Might,' she said. 'I like it up here.'

Next day we heard the chopper. Must have been following the shore, but you can hear for miles up there, it's that quiet. 'Come on,' I yelled, 'I aim to see this.' It was the weekend, the van was by the house. Suzanne jumped in behind. As we roared out the gate, Mack climbed in beside her.
'That way,' Mack guided me. We cut across paddocks till we got about up to the site. The chopper wasn't long down, the blades were still grinding to a stop. A few people were close to it. And there was Mum's cousin, that Sophie, must have come out from town. And old Sammy Kahu was easing himself off his horse, hanging on to the rope bridle. We could hear Sammy shouting at the same fulla that ordered us off that land. 'You liar, you!'
'Steady,' someone said.
'When you tell me all about this?' yelled Sammy. 'How'm I supposed to keep my cattle in when you keep flying bloody airplanes over the top of 'em all the time?'
'Calm down, Sam we can-'

'I don't pay good money to have my cattle out on that sand. Where's that fence-'
Another guy tried to push Sammy back. 'Now why not-'
'Keep out of this, Pakeha.' Sammy whirled on the guy, he pulled back smartly.
'Sammy,' said Sophie, 'this isn't the main point now-'
'It's my main point,' shouted Sammy. 'These people going to put me into the bankrupt court, they-'
'Sammy!' bellowed Sophie. 'Shut up! You've got to stop all this,' she said to the tall guy.
'That's what I just said,' Sammy put in.
'Nothing to do with your damned skin and bone stock,' she said. She shoved a letter at the guy. 'I've got lawyers' advice about this work. They're going to stop you till there's been a proper meeting.'
'What's this?' I asked Mack.
'Who'd know? Steer clear when that Sophie gets some idea into her head.'
'I won't accept this, this is nonsense,' the tall guy was telling Sophie.
I moved closer. 'Kia ora, Sophie,' I said, 'what's this?'
She didn't hear me. 'I've got lawyers, they say you can't just move in on this Crown land-'
'It has all been arranged, and properly, too,' said the guy.
'Shut it,' I told him, 'and listen to the lady.'
'What's this? You keep off this land,' said the guy.
'I go where I want, it's our land,' I said to him.
Sammy's horse was shifting restlessly, he grabbed the rope higher up.
'Not your business,' Sammy said to me. 'Just give the man the stuff, Sophie.'
She pushed the letter at him. The man didn't touch it. I grabbed it, stuck it in his pocket.
'You've got it now,' I told him.
He snatched it, threw it on the grass. 'Watch yourself!' His face splotched red.
'Don't you-'
'Keep out of this, Wiremu,' said Sophie. 'Get right out of it, don't mess this up, this is lawyer business.'
'Lawyers!' I said. 'Biggest land grabbers-'
'Wi!' called Mack, 'dry up.'

Sophie was picking up the letter. 'Our lawyers, they're getting on to your lawyers. It says in the Act you've got to-'
'Too late. It's all wrapped up now,' said the guy. 'We did it with-'
'We've got a right to our say-'
'You think you-'
'Belt up, son.' Sammy was working hard, quietening his horse. The tall guy and me, both, shifted. 'You stop your work here, layoff for a bit, or we'll get the law on you, I reckon that's what the letter says.'
'Have our share in this-' said Sophie.
'We certainly shall not, we-'
'You, you think you-'
Suzanne's voice came in. 'Over here, Wi, we're off.'
The guy was backing. 'What's all this? What do you think you're going to do? Hey, get that horse away, it's out of hand.'
'You see what bloody planes do,' said Sammy, 'all the time.'
'Nothing to do with that helicopter, it's this-'
I closed on him. 'OK, move it. You heard the man. This place, we don't want none of your messing us up, and-'
'And we don't want you in on this one, boy, I'm telling you one last time.'
'Oh, so you don't eh, just-'
'Wiremu, butt out!'
The other guys from the chopper were all around us. The pilot flashed his teeth, just like the other day. I shoved towards him.
'Hold it right there, everyone.' It was a cop. Another was helping Sammy ease his horse back.
'In good time, too, officer,' said the tall guy.
'I'll ask you all to move off, please,' said the cop, taking no notice of him.
I was off, walking down the paddock.
'Now, what's going on here, sir?' I could hear him saying to the guy.
'We're here in response to a call about a trespass.' The beach was nearest, I went that way.
'Just a minute, sir.' The other cop came in front of me. 'I think it might possibly be you we had a call from the city about, a while back. Will you just come with us, there's a few questions. '
I looked quickly around. The cop's mate was right by me.

There was a third one over the paddock. Not a sign of Suzanne, Mack. Sammy was taking his horse through the gate. The cop kept his hand off my shoulder.
'I wouldn't run, I'd just play it cool and sensible.'

I sat in the back seat by one of the cops, windows down, the sun was overhead. A cop was finishing his talk with Sophie and the tall guy, backs to us. Sophie and the guy shook hands. The chopper's blades began their spin.
We drove slowly over the grass, the bumps bouncing us hard. I saw the van, parked in the scrub. I leaned past the cop to look. Mack and Suzanne, together. No eyes, ears for anything else.
The cops were relaxed, chatty.
I clamped my jaw. Sat silent, stared down that long, empty, dirt road ahead.

ALASKAN IDYLL

Charlie Kahklen the cook just has to prove it one more time he's a dumbass. When everyone else is in the refectory had interpreted that these are English voices (Yairss), the Tlingit clunkhead goes to this one guy from the visitors who has been sat down with me and Nicky, and enquires, "Hey, are you an Eskimo? An Indian maybe?"

"Oh come on," I say embarrassed.

"Fraid not," returns the guy. "Me, I'm Maori, from New Zealand."

"Well, it just looked like you could've been," says Charlie and goes out shaking his head, maybe to check if there's any brains in it.

The guy looks at our faces and laughs. "It's ok," he says, "he's seeing my Chinese granddad in my face. No, really, I'm quite proud he thought that I might've been Indian or Inuit."

"Sure," I say. Well you've got to be courteous, they're always telling us that here.

"Yeah," he says, "but you – I've got it right? – you really are -?"

"Eskimo," I tell him, and I try my darnedest so he won't hear my jaws grit.

Because if there's one thing gets up your nose here, it's the visitors, interminably the visitors. You get lucky and it's not long till they're off with the faculty to have their talk about us kids at Tongass High (named for the National Park – look, if you're interested, go read up on it.) You see, it's the same invariable things they ask you. I mean it gets to you, it feels as if you're in a zoo. They come, they look you over, enter your classrooms maybe, take their notes and burst their camera flashes in your face. And they start with the questions. Why the Admin can't have all that stuff ready on a hand out, who'd know? It's that we're the natives, we're the representatives of all this State's aboriginals has them going, us Aleuits and Athapascans and what else all together in this residential school, and I guess maybe we're the only ones they'll ever get to meet. (You're bored already? Good! You're getting the feeling!) You'd think these people'd figure it out, but they assume, all of them, we've come all these thousands of miles (believe it!) to this town down south on the Panhandle here, and yet we're still the Eskimo, the Indian kids the same as if we'd stayed home.

This guy with us (you know, when he shuts his mouth he almost could pass himself off as some kind of Indian) has got to the, "What will you do when you leave school?"

"I'm going to train for a lawyer."

"That's great," he informs me.

"You think so?" I've got my smile nailed up good and tight.

"I do," he says. "I bet Alaska's like my home country, you need as many lawyers of the indigenous peoples as you can get in order to keep something of your own out of the hands of the government and the big corporations."

"I guess," I say. "But that's not my thing. I'm off down the lower 48 states, I'm going to practise down there when I've got my degree."

I don't want to be asked again the why, I want to turn the talk away from my privacy. He says nothing, looks at me.

It's beginning to register that this guy is killing Nicholas Perotrovich. Nick's all this time trying to push his legs against mine, have us thinking back to the other night. I don't want to have to, I'm pulling my legs away till I'm just about sitting out on air. A grin ghosts the guy's lips. He's onto what's going on under the table. "Your name's Russian?" he asks Nicky. And Nicky leans from me, spreads it for him: the Russians, the Aleuts and all of that. I think I see that the guy knows it already, but he sits and hears, looks me in the eye, and well, I'm thinking that for once, at last, here might be someone who can see us as *us*, who's ok. And suddenly it's his group's goodbye time. The guy rises, nods at us, goes. And we students head out back to do the chores and then to our rooms.

"Some view you have."

It's him, waiting in the little room that's mine. (I'm a senior, I get to have a room to myself.) He's holding the seal-bone carved to a Sedna, staring out the window where, if you crack your neck, you glimpse those shark fin mountains beyond the town, their snow spilling down them.

"What's this?" He shows the Sedna.

"Someone gave it to me, there's a story on the card goes with it."

"I get the feeling it might be quite some story," he says, stroking the glare-eyed figurine. "You can tell it? You have the time?" He's not going to tell me why he's here.

It's a story I like, so, "Just," I choose. "There's this woman, she's pretty young, really, Sedna. She's with a man, they're voyaging in his umiak – I don't know why they're travelling – and the sea gets up rough. They're about to founder when the guy hears it from the spirit that he's to throw the woman overboard, she's his Jonah."

"He does. She hangs on so tight to the side of the craft that she's going to tip him out too. He grabs his knife, he saws on her fingers till they drop off one by one. Sedna sinks to the sea's rock bed and – surprise – she cannot drown.

"She reaches for her severed sinking fingers. She finds she has in her now the magic to shape them to sea otters, walruses, seals, for she has become not a woman only but also a kind of goddess. And by her power over the creatures she's made, she has the power over the people in her old world to feed them or starve them. She's become the one whom that man and all people from then on will have to rely on. Her temper will rule their lives, and from then on only the shamans can even try to foretell what she's going to do.

"Hey, that sounds like a real Eskimo legend," he says.

"Who knows?" I tell him, "not me."

"Look," he puts the bone down. "Tomorrow, can you be free? The group I'm with is taking off to Juneau. But I want to have a longer look around Sitka. Would you consider being my guide? Or have you plans already? School will be finished tomorrow, won't it?"

"Yes." I decide to decide. "I've no plans, sure, why not show you the place?"

"Oh that's great," he says, "thanks. See you tonight."

"Tonight?" I check I've got him right.

"Of course. Wouldn't miss attending your class graduation, your – your – Baccalaureate this evening for anything, be a new one for me. See you." And he's gone.

Eight o'clock exactly and we're processing down the auditorium aisle, boys in red academic gowns, girls in yellow, and we slow pace pace pace onto the stage, with the school band roaring, it's hell on your ears. But we're solemn, dignified, look impressed with ourselves. If we didn't, we'd be waggling fingers and pulling faces at the people as if we're little kids, because we share it again, the zoo feeling. The crowd of people have come from town to honour us (knowing our families can't be here from their corners of Alaska), and eyes everywhere are staring intent, interested. Well, the show is impressive in its way, it seals us who have stayed till school's end to our new lives, it declares that the long, tough, lonely climb from home has been accomplished. The ceremony's over quickly. (There's more in the school year book if you want it.)

Hone ("You say it right Kathy") gets us a cab the next morning. And Nicky wants along too. (He's another one putting off heading back to the family for a day or two.) Hone side-rails him smooth and gentle, and we wave to Nicky from the school gate.

Hone's fired up to see the entire town. We do it properly, start (where else?) with the cannon at the Russian fort site on Castle Hill.

"1804!" he says like it's the Sphinx or something.

Then the Russian blockhouse, which I tell you is in better shape yet than the Indian houses it looks over. And the souvenir shops where no one's knocking himself out to sell, it's not their tourist season and anyway who expects an Eskimo and maybe an Indian to buy? (Hone winks, he's wise to their shopkeeper faces.)

The names of streets light him up as if they're an historical move I'm showing him.

"Hey," he says, "Lincoln, Baranoff, Princess Maksonoff, Seward, Jeff Davis, Barracks, Monastery, Sawmill Creek – surely there's a Gold Strike some place? – it's all there in the streets."

"You walk the patterning of our souls, Inuit to all-American," I tell him.

"I like that," he says.

"You're welcome. It's a quote."

By the time we're eating on this lavish dinner he buys us, mist already is sinking the town into its dark. We grab a taxi. He says he's been billeted in a house down that long Harbour Road. We're up on the two mile mark, the four mile mark, the meter's ticking. He's got his head out the window by this time, and he simply cannot pick which place it is, they're all mist-clouded to a sameness. And the driver's got his mirror on us, squinting his Indian eyes, sure we're hunting a place to roll him. I don't want him to drop us way out here. I tell Hone a school counsellor is out of town but has a spare room any of us can use any time we want it. I direct the driver, tell him wait while we check if the place is still open. The moment we're on the sidewalk the taxi screams off into the dark.

The house isn't lit. But the slide window is unlatched, we squeeze in. I fix him a bed in an alcove at the foot of the internal stairs, make up one for me in that front room on the mattress because no more taxis are going to come out in this kind of mist. The furnace is off, it's too shivering cold to sit and talk. We go to our beds. The mist has gotten into my clothes. I peel off, rub down with a towel, find me a robe to made do with, roll up in the blankets. Cold and cold rides in. My skin stokes a sweat, but no way can I feel warm. I startle.

"Kathy, this cold, I can't take it."

I let him in by me, what else to do? He feels skin, he's shucking his own gear, and we're squeezing goosebumps to goosebumps.

Morning, he brings me coffee, hot. I shudder only some to sit up.

"I've lit the furnace," he says. He sits, and the morning sun in this curtainless room shapes him more Indian – Inuit even – than I'd realised. He's staring, gazing till it seems I'm conscious of every part of me, can feel the move of my flesh, the sensing of my skin. I gulp at the coffee. Feeling, like the liquid on my tongue, scalds.

It's the museum he wants to visit next. I show the one old-time thing can draw me. It's a suit for a young kid, it's of translucent seal gut, it's delicate, it's beautiful, and you see stitched right there in its every part a people's whole Sedna-will to survive.

"You're proud!" he says.

I laugh. "Not of stuff that far back."

It has set his mind jumping. We sit out on the hard-top in the shelter of the sea wall, look over the marina to the islets of the harbour.

"This village you were born in, do you remember much of it?"

"A few flashes is all, I wasn't even going to school when I left."

"Any you can share?" He really wants it. "Just to give me the feel of the place?"

"Well, my clearest recollection, I can never figure why, is of me standing on the top step outside the house, it's a wooden step that's warped itself to cracking so that it's not a very sure foothold in that heavy wind for a little girl. I know that I'm being bad, though nobody else knows it yet – I'm standing in my indoor clothes, and the cold is rushing to my ears, my cheeks are hardening up it's so freezing cold, the wind's pouring down my lungs. But my backside's warmed by the gush of air fountaining from the house. I won't shut the door, won't go in." It's so vivid cold tears start as if from the wind in the eyes of that way back little kid. "I think I'm trying to find out how much of this I can take. I concentrate upon a grey speck moving in from where the snow has packed to ice at the coastline. A storm's rising, and I know it's my father I'm watching, stagger through the gusts. Behind him the white goes up and up to sky's white.

He thinks. "That's a good one. In a way it squares with the feeling I got from the seal-gut thing."

We walk home. In the end I have to ask him, "What's all this Inuit stuff to you?"

And he says, "Perhaps just that I can recognise so much of your past in my own background – and oh, yes, of your present too."

I want him to leave it, I say nothing. We make ourselves comfortable in their lunge, stare out on the view – "What a location!" he murmurs – that the windows parade. "I know," he says softly, "I know you're utterly fixed on it, screwed up to making a life for yourself in the Lower States. You're a million miles in your head away from the village in the snow, girl. But there's always got to be a bit of pain, the past doesn't lie down easy, and you can't cut it off like fingers. What you were then throbs like a pain inside you, no matter what. Right?"

"Ok, ok," I say, "I don't want that talk."

He stares in my face, feels for my wrist, my hand.

Quite soon – I'm astonished, I can't get over it – it's the next day, then the next, and we're still living in this house. It's like – I don't know, like nothing I'd experienced. And we talk the days around. And we visit every part of the town, we travel every road on the island (and that's not too many), we walk, we hire cars. He's really into photography, takes good shots too. He goes into the town every day to get some printed. I pose a time or two for him for the heck of it. One or two of those I bet they don't print down town.

"Wake up!" It's him yelling. Something's wrong? It's barely dawn. "Stir up, you'll miss the cab."

"Huh?" I fumble into some gear. He's ready with anoraks and stuff from the closets. "What's up?"

"Sailing," he says.

The cab drops us by the locked gates which block off the marina. He puts his hand over the wall that drops to the waves, hauls and a rubber

dinghy bounces there. "Hop in, let's choose us a launch." He's throwing our things down into the dinghy.
"You'll take a boat?"
"Of course not, borrow, share, give back in good shape, why not? It's only weekend sailors they have here. Coming, girl?"
I crawl over and slide down the rough stone. "You mustn't"
But he has a launch picked out, we're coming up alongside, gently.
"Watched them fill her up yesterday," he explains. "Greenhorns, they forgot to secure their doors."
The craft is new, yellow and white, sleek, slender. "What do you say to a turn down the harbour and along the island? Be just great this time of morning. What do you reckon?"
"You can't do this."
"So you said. Grab."
I coil the rope. He shoves the boat off, leaps aboard. The bow swings and we're drifting into the channel. He jumps down into the cabin. The motor guns.
"Just a souped up car engine, this." He's grinning. Noise avalanches onto the quiet town. I watch the shore anxiously. No one comes.
"Hone –"
"Do you want to go back?"
I shrug, I'm too confused to know. He revs the engine. An eagle bucks from our sound high into the cool air. He wraps his big goosedown anorak about us both, we join hands on the wheel, the boat noses the long smooth rollers close to the fir forest shorelines. A fishing boat's out as early as us, the two guys wave us Hi. All the rest of the morning the lumber mill down its inlet is the only settlement we see. We go isolated upon the waters between the islands as if the sea had turned to ice. We steer as we please. It is the most perfect day.
We nose to the jetty. I'm restless with feelings, I'm soft with sensation, but I sense also what I must somehow do and soon: the flight home, the new farewells, the flying to Seattle, finding a job for the summer before college commencement. I don't want to spill all this on him. I am wanting alone for a while. I leave him to take in his camera memory stick to town and I walk to the house. Since I can't seem to put into order what is inside of me, I start in to tidy the place. I flip his suitcase lid to drop some gear in. Some shorts slide. A yellow folder blazes: NZAustr-Alaska VID Corp. And *Inuit in Manhattan (working title only)*. What in hell? *Story/Direction: Hone Motu.* Inside – my fingers open it

before I can even decide – a really big colour print, a girl's head, shoulders, it's me. I have to say it, it's lovely, the face glows – yes, yes – a loving.

A page of type is clipped to it, a story, no, an outline for a movie it says, and notes and some scribbling around them. I can't read about the chief character, a girl – it's, I can't hardly take this in: it's my story, close enough. There's a date – a year ago? How? A dizziness grabs, spins me. I am the throb of my blood, none of this can be so, he couldn't have known of me back then, no, it's not possible, how could he have all that on me?

Suddenly as if a tape switches itself on in my skull I'm hearing us talking, him asking, me telling a little here, there, all that Inuit stuff, that childhood stuff, the what-am-i-heading-for-next-in-my-life stuff, all – Tundra winds lick my bone. I get it, oh do I suddenly get it! Me – I flesh his script. I am a breathing movie soft-flesh throwaway scratch pad on which to check the truth of his scripted dream. And all this, all these days, a set-up, the chance, the golden chance to pick at the body and the brain of the girl of the child I was, at my pains, my memories, me – all of me just lines, images for his cameras!

Today even, a kind of probing, a testing, to discover maybe if the will-be lawyer has the old Eskimo thiever inside of her yet! Oh man, this Inuit girl, he's sure had her wholely fooled, this dumbass fool me fool. Shame leaks, dries on my cheeks. The photo, the folder I'm ripping, I don't stop, his passport, his traveller's checks, every paper thing I find, Sedna dangerous, I'm only starting with these.

HEI AHA

A lady teacher I don't know comes smiling out of his office. The narrow strip of brightness she emerged from narrows, vanishes. My waiting starts again.
The bulb beside the door flashes green like a traffic light. I try to shut the door quietly as I go in. He's sitting back, erect as usual behind a desk spread with papers. He looks at me. He doesn't say a thing. I sit. He waits for me to tell him what he knows - why I'm here.

"So what's your problem, girl?" Dad has asked again this morning. "Hop over to the school. See him. Don't worry. It's all right if you go back to school for another year. We'll manage. Or you can try the dole for a while. Whatever you decide, it's ok with me."
"Not the dole! Not after all that school!" I'd said.
"Then see the man!"

The slits of sunlight through venetians blank out his glasses. But I know why he's silent. He'll be seeing like a video all those times I've been in here over the years.
Like last year.
Rude! That's what he'd told me the people said, and the teachers, too. Because after my big voice saying so often that we seniors ought to go down to the local marae and meet with the people there, I was the one to come late when we finally went. I don't know, it just happened. Coming down their path I'd heard the singing. I knew the welcome had started. I couldn't enter in the middle of it, not by myself.
Crockery clashed in the dining room close by. Could they do with a hand? It might be good, it might be better, working in there with them, talking, finding out some of things I wanted to know. A few tired-looking women were working non-stop. I moved forward between the close-packed trestle tables. "Hey you!" I jumped. She sounded wild! I looked up, let her see my face, my eyes. "Outside!" she said. I went closer to her. "I want to help." "Help!" Sarcasm twisted her lips. "We've been at this since six this morning! That's when the help begins!" "I know what you want," another of the women said. Others were nodding, not pausing a moment in their work. "There's always some kid who has to try to beat the rest to the food." "Not me!" I said.

"I really do want -" "Out!" the first one repeated. She glared her eyes at me.
She could see I was wanting to explain. She turned her back. I was so angry I barged out between the tables, not caring if I knocked things to the floor! "You can keep the lot of it, then, you - you cows!" I only muttered it. How come they listened to that?

"Yes, Hinewai?" he suddenly says. His mouth is a straight impatient line. I recognise the look. It's the same as that personnel man had. His finger nail had tap tapped on my school reports and papers. He'd looked up at me when I'd been shown in, and I'd thought, "Yes! I'm making contact." I felt good. I'd dressed smartly, just as the school counsellor had told us to. I started to explain the testimonials I'd brought along. I noticed his eyes. He wasn't really listening, he was looking me over! I shut my mouth in the middle of a word. He didn't notice. He said, "I have to be frank. I've already seen twenty girls with qualifications like these or better."
"But there's more," I told him. "I've had experience in the school office." "So's everyone," he murmured. "Yes, but - see? - they say how good I am at dealing with the public-" He shook his head. "Our clientele," he said. "What?" He didn't explain. His lips had fallen into that line. His eyes had closed, he rubbed at them.
The features of his face sagged as if he was bored to dying and wasn't going to hide it. Well, I'd save him! I jumped up, I shovelled my papers off his desk into my bag. He looked up in surprise. I walked out.
"Have a nice day!" the receptionist called. "Ah, shut up!" I said. The glass doors hissed slowly together. You couldn't even slam them!

"Another year as a senior?" he's saying as if it's a new idea. We sit in the silence again. I'm reassuring myself. He does have to take me, doesn't he? This isn't trying for a job. This is our school!
My thoughts won't stay still. Suddenly I'm remembering Wi thumping on the classroom windows.
"Hey! I want to see Hinewai," he called in. "Enquire at the office," Miss told him. "You can't come hammering at the window like that!"
"But she's only sitting there, see?" He pointed at me. I frowned at him, waved him away. The teacher ignored him, starting writing again on her blackboard.

He yanked the window wide, poked in a hand to summon me. "I'm heading North," he whispered. "Hinewai, sit down!" Miss ordered. "You coming with me?" "When?" He looked surprised. "Now." "Hinewai! Sit down!" “I've got to go, talk later," I whispered. He took no notice. “Make your mind up," he said. "How can I take off just like that?" He shrugged. “Hinewai!" said the furious voice. "And you - get away!" “So, see you some time," he said. “Wi?" I called. He didn't turn. I apologised to the teacher. She was scarlet-faced and breathing hard. I wondered if maybe she'd felt a little scared back there. "He seems rough but he's harmless," I tried soothing her. She wouldn't listen. She sent me to this man in his office. “I had thought that you were growing up," he'd said, “maturing, deciding what you wanted out of life." "But - " "And you know that it's absolutely against the rules for that sort of a person to be on the school grounds." "I didn't know he - Anyway, he's not ... "

What was the use? The man wouldn't want to understand. "Get back to class." I went to the common room. I didn’t want all of them seeing how I felt.

“A fifth year it would be,” he’s saying. How can I explain it to him? That I’m simply wanting to get something out of all those years at school, that’s all? And it could be this year I’ll really do well. He’s sitting there not talking again. He sighs quietly. He opens his mouth. And I can’t any longer doubt what it is he’ll say.

I should be used to it by now. I’m a fool. I always let it get to me when the people say their No. Well, I won’t just sit here, not this time! I don’t have to hear it! I stand. I tell him. “I’ll say it this time! No! I’ve changed my mind. I don’t need your school!” I catch a glimpse of myself in his blank glasses, a little far off figure. I take no notice as he starts to speak. I push shut his door.

"Hei aha!" That's what Dad would say. "Never mind!" Then he'd do this shrug. Yes. But - what now? Where do I fit in?

THE JOB

I knocked on the door and entered the room. A young lady was sitting on one of the chairs.
"Hullo," I said, "I have come about the job in the newspaper."
"Hullo," she said, "sit down on a chair and wait."
I sat on a chair.
I said to her, "Are you the receptionist?"
"No," she said, "I am not the receptionist."
"Are you the Personnel Officer?" I asked her.
"No, I am not the Personnel Officer."
"Why are you here?" I asked.
"I have also come to ask about the job."
"Oh!" I said.
A man was opening a door, I was sure that he was the Personnel Officer.
"Excuse me," I said to the young lady, "is that your car outside?"
"Yes," she said.
"I think the window is down," I said.
"Oh no" She jumped up. "Someone will steal my car!" She ran out of the room.
"Hullo," I said to Personnel Officer. "I have come to ask about the job in the newspaper."
"Where has the young woman gone?" he asked.
"She does not want the job," I said to the man.
"Okay," he said. "I will give the job to you because you are the only person here."
I was very happy. I now had a job.

MISS BICKLEY

As we come through the door we are trying to work out how Miss Bickley is today. We are, most of us, very worried about our teacher. Especially me. I am what she calls her Right Hand Man. I am her monitor. I am the one who fills in the class roll for us, who runs her messages. Today she is not too bad. The tears are oozing down her face slowly, like fat drops of rain on window glass, but she is still writing on the blackboard. We sit and begin to copy the work into our exercise books as she continues to write, the chalk making its scratchy sound. Sheryl, at the next table to me and my friend, says, "Why does she keep on crying? Why does she do it in front of other people all the time?" She asks something like that just about every day. "Shut your mouth," I tell her. "Yes! Shut up," my friend backs me up.

"Why does our teacher keep on crying?" I ask my mother that night. "I'm sure you exaggerate," she says. "Make me a cup of tea and bring it in to me. I'm off to bed." "Why can't Sharon do it?" I say. "She's the girl of the house." "You know why," she says, "she's gone to bed already. You're the oldest, you get it." "That teacher really does cry, Mum," I tell her as I bring the cup to her. But Mum isn't interested.

"Maybe someone's died," says Frank "Hey, yeah, someone she loves, eh," puts in Sheryl. "Be quiet," I tell her, "mind your own business." But my friend and I look at each other wondering if Sheryl is right. Today every now and then while Miss Bickley explains our work to us, she suddenly gives a sob and snot bubbles in her nose. Her big tits heave up and down under her blouse. I glare around at the boys until each of them looks away. We watch Miss Bickley leave the room for morning tea. "Hullo," she greets Miss Brownlow, and smiles and talks with her as they walk along the path together. "Miss," Frank asks Miss Brownlow later, "has someone died that Miss Bickley knows?" "Died? Not that I know, why?" "I think maybe she's sad," Frank explains. Miss Brownlow frowns at Frank "She seems quite her usual self to me," she answers. "But she cries a lot," says Frank. "If she has any problems she wants anyone else to know about she will tell us," says Miss Brownlow. "And she certainly would not want pupils talking about her behind her back" She stares at the small group of us boys with hard cold eyes.

"Those teachers don't know anything," says Harry watching her stride away.

"No," says Mum, "not over there. Put the cup here where I can reach it." "That teacher was crying again today," I tell her, "all the time we were in her room." "Weren't you behaving yourselves?" asks Mum sharply. "I've told you never to cause trouble at school!" "We weren't. I've told you, she's always crying. And when she goes outside the room she's ok again. It's creepy." But Mum is saying, "Wait, Joe, while I drink this." "I'm tired," I tell her, "I want to go to bed." "Won't hurt you to wait," she says. "Go on, sit down, there."

"What is the date today, Joe?" She knows that I have pasted a page with the calendar on it into the front of my exercise book. I check it again. "It's the 21st, Miss," I say. Suddenly Miss Bickley sits at her table and hides her face in her hands. Her shoulders shake as she cries. "Must be," says Sheryl with satisfaction in her voice as if no one could disagree with her now, "must be someone in her family has died." None of us say anything. We don't know what to say or think. I stare down at my calendar. Its four weeks till Dad comes home. I have marked it in red, the date that Mum said he'll return. Perhaps he'll understand what's wrong with Miss Bickley. Miss Bickley stands. She begins to tell us what our next work will be. Her tears slowly dry on her face.

"This teacher you're always talking about," says Mum, "I suppose she's young and good looking, and starting her first job?" "No she isn't." I try to describe Miss Bickley. "Her hair has grey like bits of cobweb caught up in it. She hardly wears any make-up at all and you can see where her cheeks look as if they're going soft and shrinking in. I think she's been at our school for a long time." "Tell the truth," says Mum. "I am," I tell her. "Give us a good night kiss," says Mum. "Miss Bickley -" "Oh, for heaven's sake, let's not talk about her again," says Mum. "Turn out the light." "You'll go sleep?" I ask.

The headmaster comes into the room. We look up. All the quiet chattering stops. Miss Bickley turns around from the blackboard. "Oh, Mr Forester," she says, "you startled me." She laughs. "I must have a guilty conscience," she goes on, "that's what my mother always used to say when something made us jump." "Sorry," he says. "I wondered if some of your class could deliver these newsletters around the school." "I'm sure they will." "I'll leave them here then." He looks at the work on the board, and glances around at us. "Are they working well, Miss Bickley?" "They're a very good class," she says. We stare silently back at him. I see that Miss Bickley is still smiling as if she's happy. The headmaster smiles back at her. I feel really peculiar, as if I'm in a dream. How can she suddenly be smiling like that? And him, can't he see the wet crumpled tissues in the wastepaper tin, the swollen eyes she turns on him? Can't he tell anything? Won't she speak to him about what is making her cry all the time? Is it us, this class? Is it me, her Right Hand Man? Have I done something? Does she know-? No that's stupid. Is there anyone who can help her? The headmaster goes out the door. Right away her tears begin to leak from closed eyelids. She dabs at them with a tissue. Should I go after the headmaster, ask him to return and talk with Miss Bickley and get her to explain these tears? "Joe." She is standing in front of the blackboard again, her hands twisting together. "Please hand around the newsletters. Go and deliver them to the other classes, all of you, now." I look back as I leave. She sits slumped, head resting on the teacher's table.

My mother reaches past me and switches off the bedside lamp. The room is dark. The heavy curtains are pulled tight across the window. "Mum, is Dad still coming home next month?" I ask. "Who knows?" she answers, pulling aside the duvet.

"What will I do?" cries Miss Bickley as she stands in the middle of the classroom between the rows of tables. "How do you mean, Miss?" Sheryl asks. Miss Bickley ignores her. The tears begin their rain-drop trails down her cheeks. She walks to her own table, sits. "Miss, has your mother - ?" Sheryl begins. "Belt up," I tell Sheryl. "I don't like this class anymore," says Sheryl, "I don't like coming here at all." I can't think of anything to say. I can't concentrate on the work in the book that Miss Bickley has given us. Usually I can do this work easily. I don't know what is wrong with me.

"Cold?" she murmurs. I don't answer her. She doesn't care if I do or not. Her hands move. Her skin is warm. Her hair spills onto me, dark hair with no grey in it, heavy hair that touches down to my shoulders. I pull back my head to say, "Mum!" But I can't stop it happening, I can't, not ever.

Miss Bickley hardly cries at all through the day. Only once does she give a huge sob. But I can't do the work. The questions that the book is asking are too hard for me to understand today.

"Go to bed, Joe," Mum says. "You'll sleep well now. Goodnight." I say nothing. As I run from her room I hear her whisper, "Shh or you'll wake the others." I get into my bed. Its cold, I shiver. I stare in the moonlight at the calendar on the open page of my book.

There is no one in the classroom when we arrive. We all stand around the room talking. Frank and Harry push the tables together so that they can play pingpong. I sit wondering if I should do something. The door opens and the principal walks in. Everyone hurriedly sits at a table while he waits for us to be silent. "Class," he says, "Miss Bickley has had to go away to er - a hospital." "She's sick, sir?" asks Sheryl. "Yes," says the headmaster, "she's very sick." "Is that why she was crying every day?" Sheryl wants to know. The headmaster frowns at her. But he does not look angry, he looks as if he finds all this very hard to say to us. "I think so. We - I have only just realised that she has been sick for some time. Not sick physically, not the flu or anything. It's more a sickness of the mind. She's been under a lot of strain, you see." He says no more. But I know what he is telling us. He is saying that we have made her sick. "I want you to wait very quietly for a few minutes while I find a teacher to take you. No noise at all." As soon as he goes out Sheryl speaks. "Told you! I said something really was wrong with her!" "Shut up!" I say to her. But I say it quietly. I don't know if she hears me. I don't care. I don't listen to what my friends are saying about Miss Bickley. I'm concentrating so much on wondering - was it me? Did she find out the truth about me and what happens in the darkness just about every night? Was that her strain? Was she ashamed to know of it, and to have to face me in her class every day, to have me still as Her Right Hand Man? "Hey, Joe? Joe?" But I can't listen to them. I am thinking these same thoughts over and over.

"Mum? You know that teacher who cried? Well, she's gone crazy, the headmaster said, she's had to go away. Do you think -" "Maybe she's had a very sad life," says Mum. "Who knows? Don't worry about her." "'Mum, will Dad be home next week?" "Uh-uh," she says shaking her head. I switch out the light. I stand there a moment, I can't stop thinking about Miss Bickley. I can't stop thinking about how bad I am. "Joe?" says Mum impatiently. I move, as I always do, towards her bed.

CAN'T YOU LISTEN

Don't you ever want to hear me? My speaking you want stomped on, shut up, put down? Hey, hey, I'm speaking to you, yes, you all you teachers, pigs, it's you, Plunket Nurses, bosses, storekeepers, all you office sitters, people pushers, all of you the same. You, none of you - and I don't know why - listen.

No, not new, nothing of that is new at all. But what's new is how it's got to this: in me there's like some great bird, some albatross eagle condor, its wings stretching out, beating, strength building, wanting to burst out of the flesh of me. But nah, scratch that, it's just from some - what? - movie, doesn't catch how I feel it. The fact is that there is this voice that's, well yes, that's growing in me and is wanting to speak, to cry out. No matter where, no matter who's there, what's going on, it tries to crank at my tongue, work at these lips. It starts deep in my belly, a long quiver of sound that only I hear. It sucks in a lungful of air to itself. And I have to clamp hard on my jaw, turn the sound that's starting out, twist the lips its shaping into a cough. I've managed. So far.

Thing is, I don't know, I can't work it out what the voice is wanting to shout. I know, I just know, that if this voice gets its word out then everything'll go smash, be changed. Me too, I won't be the same again. Because the voice could shatter my world and there'll be something so different I'm scared even to think of it how it could be.

It's at this place, this Institute place, the voice's power grows. I really have to fight it down. I shove it back into my larynx. I squeeze it inside my gut. Ignore its burning, working in there as if it's something solid. (Oh, they were so keen when I was at school for me to get into this place!) And I think it's because it's especially these people here, don't ever hear me. They all the time seem to be trying to hear the girl they want to think they're making of me. To hear the echoes in me of the things and the ways that they've spoken at me.

Nobody knows how I'm feeling, no one back at home, even my one or two mates who've made it here they seem somehow able to hack it. But me, I can't.

This deafness around me works on me all of the time. I don't know how to tell it, I sense as if their eyes are on me, their mouths say at me, grin at me, but none of them see ME. If my words come honestly out of me, they can't make themselves listen - they can't seem to hear what they don't expect. If I say as it comes, as I feel, if I ask what I'm wanting to know their eyes seem to glide as if my sentences were building doorless walls which they can't peer over.

It's more, it's as if I, as if myself am a book in a language they can't, they won't understand. Where I'm coming from, the fact that I'm not sure where I'm headed, seems to make for them a plot they can't read. And they can't Dewey Number me to the shelves inside their heads. There's no getting to them, there's no meaning in me that to them is significant.

It's getting worse, oh worse than at school, they (you, alright, you) are much more impatient or some such here. (Am I making some sense, are you getting any of this at all?) It's got so that I can't concentrate on all you're saying and saying, it's cry out oh God no I'm clenched lip upon them cry their iron rod has struck belly's fountain spirit's welling struck to rock dry shut up this is purely gibberish where does such stuff come from? The flame of the heart shall burn them God that is my uncle's voice, Tu's, the one who's dead. No, it's like some preacher, someone I must've heard, a movie, yes a sound-track of a voice. It's trying again to yell with my mouth pump my chest. They're looking. I have to get out of here - I'm scared - out of this place. (But where to?) This is not my fault. I don't, I don't choose this.

One day, sure, I'll know what my voice inside is waiting to tell. And then, ok, I know I'll be able to spill it, I'll scream it out. You'll see, one of these days it'll have to happen. And then you'll whakarongo mai, oh, how you'll all listen!

IN THE KIWI HOUSE

In the kiwi house it is beautiful. The light is dimmed, easy on old eyes shrinking from Summer's glare. There is never a jostling of people. The watchers are usually quiet, even in their delight when their eyes adjust and they see the creatures in their simulated night time among the vegetation and the branches. The people seem contented, even gentled by what they see. It is seldom one finds such a place of good humour, good nature, good hearted easy companionship.

Today there are only children here, two little girls, each eating a large white ice-cream. The lights in their places between the glass cases catch and polish their smooth rounded limbs, glint their eager eyes. One jumps back with a tiny scream of shock as a large headed weta extends his antennae towards her. "You can see, can't you," I tell her, "They are behind their glass? Go on, touch the window, it's safe. Now come, look at these, you'll like them better," taking her hand I lead her to the kiwis. Her smile grows as she watches the active one plunge his bill again and again into the rotting log immediately before the pane. He leaps to reach as high as he can, exposing each time one long pale skinny leg just like some plump slatternly middle-aged woman in a dress too short for her. The other bird remains at rest in a far corner, shadowed from the lamp light. But I can see him clearly. I watch him break out from under the bush between the two dogs, run swiftly, run amazingly swiftly and my high voice cheers him on until he dashes among the fallen timbers, and the dogs are left to sniff and sniff and won't admit that he's eluded them. I laugh, the girls laugh with me. Noreen, when she was oh ten or twelve, had perfect yes perfect legs, all summer bared to the curve of buttock. It is a rare gift a strange gift, anything perfect. (All I can see of me in her is the spill of fine, dark hair.) The little girls are going. It will be close to lunch-time. I mustn't keep the wife waiting with the meal, she gets so irritated. "Thank you Noreen," I call. I don't think she remembers me from when they were living next door so long ago. She can't hear. She is rushed off her feet by a crowd waiting for tickets to the kiwi house or to buy the T-shirts or tea towels or the brown Easter-egg chickens with foolishly long bills pasted onto their faces and thrust slap-dash into cracked wide eggshells, or the other grotesque things the place has to sell.

I hurry along the road - I'm an old fool! Natalie has passed away. She has been gone - years it must be. Will there be anything at home to eat? I can't recall, tap my pockets, check that I am carrying money. I notice a cafeteria, turn in to eat there. "Morning," says the assistant, "the usual for you today?" The familiarity of the woman! What on earth does she mean? I move along, choosing from the plates behind their plastic display hatches. But she is already picking out sausage rolls, cream cakes, placing them on a plate before I can ask for them. "I'll thank you to let me choose for myself," I tell her. "And a pot of tea too, please." She is already putting that on the tray as well.

I sit in the corner away from the street. The girl called Reena? Ina? Wasn't at the kiwi house again today, it's been a while. Perhaps she's out of town. Indeed I think it might be the school holidays since so many youngsters are on the streets all day long. She regards me as a sort of uncle. She seems a solitary, a lonely child, like me enjoys to visit the place. She loves to pretend to think that the creatures are really in a natural terrain, that the struggle for survival takes place in there, that they risk hurt, move in fear of predators. She likes to have her shoulder squeezed, to share the knowing then that there's really no call for scare. She too has a fall of dark hair, she once let me an instant stroke even - there's however nothing of Noreen to observe in her.

It's not good sitting here, though, unemployed like this. I can't remember at all how it could have come about. I've always been a good worker, given an honest day's labour. I don't fancy the idea of sitting here during working hours, watching others who are occupied. I'll have to take steps to secure employment. The unemployment can't surely be so bad as the newspapers present. It was terrifying - the kiwi house is a place of peace. The lights of a sudden all flickering on and off not precisely in tandem which makes the flaring of illumination so much harder to bear. They blow out altogether. It is as if the place is ascending at speed like one of those vertical take-off hawker jets. My knees are scarcely able to sustain my weight. I fall against the glass of the kiwi lair, my fingers scratching and sliding for a purchase on the glass plate. The children next to me hang onto me tight, eyes giant with terror. The active bird is opening his bill, calls to me piteously, jerking his head to and fro in his agony. The morepork is clinging flat to his perch. The room spins, there is a roaring, a sensible thrumming as of a motor. I can fill my lungs only in great spaced out gasps. The motion of the place is a vertigo of pain. The moment I can, I make my way out, using the surfaces of the glass to ease my steps. I can hardly see. I am sweating. I sit out on the concrete retaining wall of the garden. I see the crowd milling along the street and in the park as usually, no damage has been done. Surely it must have been a highly localised earth spasm from somewhere deep where the subducting rock merges to the mantle? Or perhaps it is a deceitful structure, the octagonal kiwi house. Perhaps those strange spires conceal some drive power that can shift, can elevate the floor at random intervals? Ha! Now there's an idle mind's humour! (Yet that moment of horror, it leaped in me exactly yes exactly like the jump-jet!)

Abruptly I see it perfectly - the personnel officer handing me the set of albums for photographs. A bright orange cover they had, somewhat vulgar actually. But we are polite, we because Natalie is there, she wears a hat from some sense of occasion. And I make a graceful speech of thanks for this retirement gift, though afterwards at home Natalie is bitingly scathing of such a cheap and undesired gift after so many decades with the department. In the winter the kiwi house is very quiet, not busy at all, pleasantly warm. I remember that time of bitter wind, off the mountains, the snow-chill of it getting right to the marrow. And that American woman - what an absurd outfit! Whoever could have advised her on what was suitable for our climate? Bare feet in sandals in that kind of weather! She kisses me and says, "Thanks, Pops," and tells me I've explained the natural habitat of the kiwi so clearly, and pointed up such interesting parallels between apteryx australis and archaeopteryx. I remember to respond to her, "You're welcome." A lovely little child she had with her, but wouldn't come near, wouldn't say a word.

That photo album, I wonder where it is? I'll have to ask Natalie. She cannot ever clean the house without a wholesale moving of things, every spring clean (and how brief the seasons of her housekeeping!) it's as if we've shifted house. Their arms and legs are so warm, so intrinsically glowing it is utter aesthetic delight to touch and the little backs in swim suits and the sun dresses. "Time for us to go. Everything ok in here today, Mr Pine?" calls Noreen. She is a kindly girl, has a sweet disposition, and a sweet featured face. I enjoy to see the chase upon it of her expressions. "See you again. Are you all right to get home on your own?" "I'm fine, thank you very much, Noreen, I appreciate your allowing me in again on the house like that."Bye for now, I'll see you tomorrow." Ah yes, for here in the kiwi house, how mind can float upon its stillness, eyes' looking ease in the sympathy of the lighting. "Visiting time again." How? Who is this? "You'd like someone to pop in?" What can she mean? A whiteness. What is this, what's happening - this dazzling, this light. Why? For seeing what?

FLY AWAY PETER

There is never any love in a grey hound. They are content to be just themselves - silent, self contained, selfish and off handed. So when our father "just acquired" Peter we were not exactly thrilled. "He'll catch every rabbit on the place, see if he doesn't," our fond parent said proudly.

It was another of his grand money making schemes. He was already seeing piles of rabbit carcasses, pelts for sale, meat for eating.

Anyhow, we patted the slim ribbed dog and said animal words to him to make Peter feel at home but he just stood there, a sad, sad looking thing with a faraway look in his eyes, gazing into the distance. That dog never laughed, he couldn't even manage a smile - and we all did our best.

As for chasing rabbits? We couldn't coax him away from the house, not even with Tom, the little black fox terrier romping around him. We had to lead the grey hound to a paddock where rabbits were plentiful, almost right up to a large buck. We took the chain off Peter's collar - was the dog interested? He looked everywhere but at the rabbit, who stood a few yards away twitching his whiskers. Peter stared at the distant hills, then made a bee line for home.

This happened so many times that we all gave him up in disgust.

One day our mum gave us a "piece" each and walking many a mile, leading Peter, we climbed to a far off hilly farm where rabbits were so thick and tame anyone at all could knock them down with sticks. In no time at all our terrier Tom managed to catch seven.

But Peter, he just stood there with a look of boredom on his face, with that look of contempt in his dreamy eyes, gazing away into space. We did our best to teach him to catch rabbits - then he was off, homewards. We returned just in time to catch him trotting down the road with the week's meat supply. The family joint often went - cooked or raw, it was all the same to Peter. He had silent ways, he could enter the kitchen unseen and unheard and somehow steal anything eatable. A duck or two, a couple of laying hens were on the missing list too - Peter was suspected, but nothing could be proved against the imperturbable creature. He looked sadder and sadder and grew thinner and thinner.

And the great money making scheme was turning into a money losing one with the cost of all the missing food. Father looked at Peter. Time to cut his losses.

"You'll have to lose him," said our father. But Peter refused to get lost - he just kept on coming back. A born thief. Nothing was safe where that dog was concerned.

Father could take no more. He looked at me. "You've got us into a right mess here. It's up to you to get rid of him before he costs me another cent."

So I decided to take him out to the "valley" and lose him there. He'd never find his way back from there - just trot on and attach himself to someone new. I was doing the mail run for our Frank, so I took the greyhound with me in the cart, but Peter wouldn't run when tied behind the vehicle, didn't like riding in it either. I gave it up as a bad job when I got to the Presbyterian Church. I lifted the dog out and fastened him up to a post with a piece of string - a good hard tug and the string would break. I went on my way rejoicing and left the dog enjoying the scent of honeysuckle in the noon day sun.

I returned after my round but instead of Peter there stood old Mrs McGill, mother of 17 children, most of them adult, stalwart sons.

"So you tried to palm off that dog on to me did you?"

"No, Mrs McGill," I said. "I was only trying to lose him."

"Losing him my foot," she said. "Do you know what he's done."

"Yes," I said. It wasn't hard to guess. "Stolen your meat."

"Meat," she roared. "Meat! No, a whole whacking side of bacon - this is going to cost your dad a pretty penny or two, I can tell you."

But at least we never saw Peter again.

THE FIRST CAR AT RUATAHUNA

"No," said Nanny Paora, "my name is Renatataukua Himiona."
"But," said the man, "your husband is - "
Nanny firmly interrupted the visitor. "Te Horowai, that's his name."
"You are Mrs William Paul, aren't you," said the man in the dark grey suit, putting his cup down.
"You haven't been sitting in my house five minutes enjoying my hospitality and you are trying to tell me my name!" said Nanny.
"Your hospitality is very much appreciated," said the man.
"Yes, yes, thank you," said the pale looking younger man in the blue suit and the shirt with the funny collar. He was nearly choking on the runny buttered scone he had been putting into his mouth. It was his third scone, too.
"You don't have to thank me or appreciate it," said Nanny Paara. "You just have to expect it, Mr - "
"This is Mr Frederick Fergusson," said the man in the grey suit for the second time.
"I can't remember these pakeha names," said Nanny. "Can't get my mouth around them half the time, either. They make my dentures fall out."
Fanny gave a snort of a giggle. I frowned her to silence.
"But it is Mr William Paul who is now in Rotorua Hospital who is your husband, Mrs ... er-?"
"Yes, of course he is," said Nanny Paora. "Who else would have him? That' s just his pakeha name."
"He told us to talk with you - "
"Is he all right? Is he improving?"
"Oh yes indeed, the Sister said he was doing quite well."
"I hope you didn't let him see your car," said Nanny, "that one you've got outside my house." She poured another cup of tea all round.
"Our car?"
"Yes, he always wants the first and the best, that man. Look at him now. This flu' epidemic, it isn't so bad as the one we had right after the Great War, the Kaiser's War, a couple of years back. But him, he has to go chasing those few bony sheep of his up and down hills you wouldn't run a goat over, and in the rain too. And so he gets the worst flu' in the place and they have to send him to the Rotorua Hospital to fix him.

He'll be wanting a car like that too, you bet, if he caught even a glimpse of that one out there."
The men couldn't stop their eyes from glancing all around Nanny's bare boards little house, trying to think - you could see it in their expressions - where the money could come from to buy a car.
"I don't get to see him much. He'd only skite at me about his flu'. Anyway, the horse has gone lame."
"You'd go to Rotorua on horseback?"
"Of course," said Nanny Paora. "How else?"
There was a silence while the two men thought about little old Nanny going from near Ruatahuna to Rotorua and back on a horse.
The man in the grey suit broke the quietness. "It's really in a way about the car that we have come. You see, soon there will be many cars using the road that runs along your fence line, going from Rotorua to the coast."
"That's good," said Nanny. "They can take me to Wairoa whenever I want to go. Be good to look up the family there now and again."
"Ah, these will be private cars rather than buses or taxis. You know that the needs of cars are different from horse traffic, so that the road will have to be improved, gentler gradients located - "
"I don't know these big words," said Nanny. "Tell me what you want in simple words that I can follow."
My gaze skipped across to where lay the big old English Bible that Nanny liked to read to us from. It was just cram full of hard words that Nanny had to explain to us kids. I hoped that the men wouldn't notice.
"We want to change where the road runs. It will take only a little land - "
"I thought so!" Nanny shook her head. "A pakeha never comes to call on you these days in your house unless he's buying or selling something. It's always talking about buying or selling. Don't you ever talk about anything else? What does your wife talk about?"
The man in the grey suit looked at her, startled. "I don't know. She talks about things for the house, the housekeeping, I suppose and the chi- "
"Listen to that," said Nanny to me, "even the ladies have to talk about buying and selling! So, Mr Kemp, what land are you wanting now to buy or sell?"

The man looked angry. His face went red. "Even your prophet up in his Mountain is buying and selling land, madam," he said. "It has to be done if we're all to make a living."
"He's not my Prophet. We're Presbyterians. We farm our own land, we're not climbing up to his village, there's enough mountains here. And yet," and her eyes suddenly went dreamy, looking way way through the two men on the other side of the table, "what if Rua's vision ever came to be?" The men looked puzzled. "What land?" demanded Nanny, her eyes sharp on the men.
"Oh, er, well, it's not really buying or selling," said Mr Kemp.
"No?" said Nanny suspiciously.
"Mr Paul suggested that we negotiate with you. To swap land. You know where the surveyors laid out a line on the other side of the hill from the existing road?"
"Cheeky lot," said Nanny, "walking onto my land like that. They wouldn't get off, either. Poking their pegs into my paddock."
"I'm sorry if it upset you," said Mr Kemp. "But that marks the preferred new road. If you could give us that strip, we would return to you the land the present road is on."
"I don't want that road," said Nanny. "What good is a road like that to a farm? All that metal and stone on it? It's useless. That's a good paddock those two rows of pegs go through."
"The metal can be raked off, grass will return," urged Mr Kemp.
"Who needs a road through the middle of a farm?"
"Not quite the middle - "
“I’d have to drive my cows and my sheep across a road with cars running up and down it all day, scaring them and leaving dust from all the way to Wairoa. What a foolish idea. This is a farm not a race track You'd have every sheep so skinny from worry it'd be like shearing an empty sock."
"You would be free to use the road for stock at any time," said Mr Kemp. "The traffic would not be heavy, far from it, and we could guarantee you use of the road."
"And we'd own the present road again?"
"Yes."
"Everything on it? The metal, stuff like that?"
"Of course, if you wanted it."
"I suppose," said Nanny, "if I say no you'll come back with a policeman and tell me I've got to do it anyway." She looked sad.

"Well, not just like that, I hope, but - "
"All right. It's hard when you're old and alone like me to argue with you." None of us six mokopuna made a sound. "I'll sign."
"Oh, well done. But we'll have to return with the correct papers to - "
"No, I want to do it now. I'm worried half to death about my husband, and only these little grandchildren of mine - " my brother Timu scowled to hear the word little "- are keeping the farm going. I want it all over with, finished. You have papers, I can see them."
"Yes, but - well Mr Fergusson is a lawyer, yet it's very irregular. I don't really think that we can-"
Nanny dabbed at her eyes with the ends of her scarf. "I'm an old lady. I can't put up with all this fuss and bother and this buying and selling and swapping land. It's too much."
"But - " Dab, dab.
"Oh very well, if you - "
"Get me my pen," she told me. "Do I sign here? Now you sign for the government people. There. You too, young man. That's all done? The road is mine now?"
"Technically speaking it is, but in strict - "
"All right. Mokopuna, haria mai te hoiho," she told my next sister, Pane "- fetch the horse. Be careful, Mr Kemp and Mr Fergusson, two men is a big load for a lame horse. You can hire yourselves a horse and gig when you get to the Ruatahuna store."
"Horse?" The younger man's words squeaked.
"Well, the car on the road is mine," said Nanny.
"The car?" The young man's hands shook. His face went as white as a full moon. "You can't-"
"You signed it. Look, see? There's the signatures. The road is mine. And everything that's on it."
"That is nonsense," said the young man loudly.
"Hmmm," murmured Nanny Paora. "Well, looks like I'll have to ask my mokopuna, my grandson John, to come and have a look at those papers and sort it all out in the court. He's a lawyer too."
"You have a lawyer in the family?" The young man reached for the papers. He turned to the other man. "Sir, we'd be made to look fools for even signing it like this ..."
"Oh yes, yes," Nanny told him, "he is our lawyer, eh children."
"Of course," we said in chorus.

"He's our own legal man all right," I assured the man. John was too. He was so clever that he had to go away to school, just like his grandfather had had to go away to the hospital. He was in the third form at Te Aute College. He was studying to be a lawyer, no doubt about it.

"He will look into this for me." Nanny poked the papers towards the young man with a thin finger.

The young man got up. Some crumbs bounced down from his jacket. "This is -"

"Mrs Paul," said the older man. "I had a long talk with Mr McDonald who dealt with roading matters around here before I took over."

"A good man," said Nanny.

"He asked to be remembered to you."

"Four cups of tea," said Nanny.

"I beg your pardon?" asked the man in the grey suit.

"He always had four cups of tea, couldn't even begin to talk until he'd had four cups of tea. My husband said he must have come from Jersey or Angus or somewhere. He had an extra stomach for the tea."

Mr Kemp smiled. "Sit down, Mr Fergusson." He looked at me. "And will the young lady join us too in a friendly game?"

"What?" The young man was too surprised to be polite.

Mr Kemp pulled a pack of cards from a pocket. "Name your game, Mrs Paul."

Nanny tucked the ends of her scarf into her cardigan. "Are those cards?" she asked. "I'm not too sure about any of these card games, you'll have to be patient with an old woman." She got up, put on her head band that kept the hair out of her eyes. "What about pontoon?" she said.

"I think we all know what the stake is," said Mr Kemp.

"Brmmm, brmmm," said Timu when the young man turned an anxious face, to Mr Kemp.

The young man whispered, "You can't, the car belongs to-"

"Be quiet," said Nanny. "No talking while you play. Mokopuna, e Pane, put the horse back in his paddock."

Oh well, I thought as I looked over my cards, Grandfather Paora in the hospital would be able to tell people for the rest of his life how for a little while, for half an hour, he really did own the first car in the whole district.

THE MOUNTAIN

Near Tere's place is a mountain the locals call Patupaiarehe Mountain - Fairy Mountain. According to the old folk no one was supposed to climb it.

Whenever Tere's father heard anyone talk about that he'd say, 'Damn Maori nonsense.' But his grandmother would say to the kids: 'No, you just stay right away from that place and you'll be all right.' And she'd add, 'If your mother had been here still she'd say the same.' Well they couldn't argue about that one.

Anyway, they never did climb to the top - one good reason was that it was too hard to climb.

Every now and then Tere's father said he'd climb the mountain just to show everyone. But he never did either. He always said he was too busy on the farm, though Tere reckoned he was simply too lazy!

Even in those days the timber mills had gone from all around the area. You can imagine what sort of country it was if the saw mills and the sheep farmers had left it alone. It was all steep, rocky hills and deep gullies and scrub and bush everywhere, with the Mountain in the middle.

Well, a while back a small plane got lost in a storm and must have crashed somewhere near that mountain. So, since Tere knew the place, he took his first break from the farm since he'd left school the year before, and joined the search parties that were going over the whole area.

The searchers didn't find the plane where they thought it should have been, and the men were split into small parties - with Tere being told to act as guide for a group of three men ... up Fairy Mountain.

The climb was terrible, as bad as anything Tere had expected. And what made it worse was the wetness of the bush and the muddiness of the ground. By midday they reckoned they were only half way up the mountain.

They took a break for a feed, and stayed resting, putting off for a few minutes the start of the climb up the worst part.

Tere was looking out over the country. You'd never believe they were only a few miles from the town and even less from that big sheep station of Mr James's. The place was so quiet he could hear a few birds somewhere. And then he started to think he could hear something else, something like singing? Chanting like at a tangi or something? Couldn't be.

'I think that lad's gone to sleep again,' said John McCormick, the cop from over Opapa way, and the sheep farmer laughed and said, 'Come on, Tere boy, we've got to get down before dark, y'know.'

'Can't you hear anything?' But they couldn't.

'We got to shift. Let's move' said the cop. 'No time for Maori P.T.,' and he laughed, though in a friendly sort of way.

They climbed hard and went well till they came to a narrow ledge of flat ground, and stopped for a breather. They were happy with how fast they'd gone, and were laughing and talking, having a real good time. Tere told them about what his grandmother and the other old people used to say about this mountain they were climbing, and what his father had said. And the cop and Harry, the sheep farmer, talked about the mountains they'd climbed and the rescues they'd been on before. Tere had never felt so strongly that he was a man among real men.

They started climbing again. Between trees, suddenly, Tere saw this girl. She was a Maori all right, but her skin was light, like a Pakeha. Her hair was kind of red-brown and hung down over her shoulders. She was wearing only a little, triangle-shaped apron thing, with nothing else on. She was the most beautiful girl he'd ever seen. And she stood there leaning with one arm against a tree fern, smiling at him. All he could feel was a coldness all over. He had stopped dead.

'What's up, Terry?'

'See something, man?' asked the others.

They were looking over his shoulder. 'Can't you see?' he managed to say. But they could see nothing.

'Go on, go on, there's no wreckage here,' and John gave him a bit of a shove on the way.

They started to climb. The girl turned and went ahead, about four feet in front of Tere.

They had to climb even harder now. She still kept just ahead as if it was no trouble. Then she disappeared and Tere felt good again. As he turned his head to make a joke about what he thought he'd seen, he saw her, about 20 feet away. She was waving out from a big split running up a rock face. Just as he saw her, Harry said, 'Hey, look, there's an opening in the rock. Let's see if there's a way up to the top.'

Tere was shaking with fright. 'No, no,' he said.

'Why not?' "said John McCormick. 'You'll manage it. We'll help you up, Tere.'
And they were already heaving themselves up the slope towards the opening. Tere tried to call out to them, but he wasn't able to. He thought, If only I could crack that joke, or laugh, or sing or something I'd be all right. Then he remembered from away back - if only he had some food - some smokes - money - chewing gum even. But he had nothing left, and the others had all that was left of the food.
He was further up the slope than the others were and somehow, against his will, he found himself there first.
The girl was just inside a high cave. It was all wet smelling and the floor was slippery with leaves and moss. She smiled and beckoned him on. Behind her he could hear water falling. He stopped and braced himself against the walls to prevent himself from moving forward. He could hear the others asking what was wrong. But instead of listening to them he was listening to the water. There seemed to be a small waterfall, and the sound echoed as if the water went a long way down. And then from some part of him that he didn't know was there he knew what the girl wanted. He knew he must shut his eyes so that he could not see her and go back, outside, straight away.
'For Pete's sake, what now!' said McCormick.
'Out!' Tere seemed to have to gasp the words.
'Let me past.' And he pushed Tere against the wall and tried to squeeze past him. Eyes still shut tight, his tongue trying to find words of the old language, Tere tried to resist him. But he seemed to have no strength against McCormick. In a flash both were sliding and falling into the cave and down. Down and down in the dark, bouncing hard against rock, water all the time pouring down on them, and the roar of a creek below getting louder and louder against their screams, and a funny kind of laugh going on and on and on and ....
Harry, lying full length on the wet rock and holding hard to the knobs on the walls, stared in horror down into the now silent darkness.

THE GREAT KIWI PAINTING

I'm stunned. I jump out of the car, run disbelievingly closer to stare. Great curves of paint cross our long white house wall which faces the street. Not taggers, I can see that. I'm just getting an inkling what this is about when the front door opens and Mae rushes out beaming. "You see, dear, I've started another painting. It'll be my best."
"On the side of our home?" I croak.
"Oh yes, that's the only place for it. It'll be my best and it'll make us the most Kiwi people around. No more busybody asking how long I've been in New Zealand! Don't they listen to my Kiwi voice? Don't I look like a Kiwi?"
I stare at the baggy t-shirt and pants cut off raggedly one leg at the thigh, one at the knees, all with paint spots, and down at the purple jandals. "No," I say, "you look like someone from Mars. Or Venus."
She mock-glares at me, then takes my arm. "Don't look so worried, you wait, you'll see, it'll be something people will come to look at, trust me."
I do, of course I do … but a mural on a suburban house? And I don't care too much about other people right now … will I want to see it on our house?
Her work slowly enlarges. "Don't look," Mae instructs me every day, "I want the final thing to be a surprise."
"It's already a surprise," I assure her.
She giggles, and smoothes my brow. "Really," she murmurs, "even your cousin who keeps talking about the Treaty might like it, I'll put in some *kina.*
I sigh. "Not this again - forget her, you don't have to prove anything to anyone. You are who you are, you're my wife."
She glared at me. "I'm not same chattel you own."
"That came out wrong, you know it's not what I meant - just, just be happy."
"I am happy - happy doing this." Her momentary flare of irritation gone, she returns to the subject now dearest to her heart. "Just let the front grass grow, then you won't have to twist your neck not to look at it." And she bustled me off.

I know now how this all began.

On the train into work I think about it. That damn cousin.
"Maori have nowhere else to go," she had said when we bumped into her last week. Whenever she started on this, it always unsettled Mae, made her feel like she was an intruder, should go back to her own 'home'.
"None of us have anywhere else to go," I answered back. "This is home to all of us. We're all Kiwis now. Mae's grandfather came out here, just like my grandfather did - just like your grandfather did. We're all the same."
And there had been that sneer of the eyes, that glance. Trouble with all this resurgence of Treaty rights, in the mouths of some people, it just turns into denying the rights of others.
I'd got rid of her quick enough and we carried on, but it has been festering there.

So this is a painting about families, about lineages, whakapapa, Mae claiming New Zealand for her. Great idea. I can understand. But on the house? So of course I look whenever she's away from home. She's sticking things to the weatherboards, bits of glass, plastic, to make it maybe as if she's cut out and patched light across her painting. What'll this do to the re-sale value of this house? How will it sit with Julia and Sam next door? They complain about anything! Or those new-comers from India across the road? I can't see any of them liking something so bizarre, not straight away. I pry at a corner or two but the tiny pieces are firmly attached. Every day I fret about it, quietly, not wanting to put the artist off. She's so confident when she's busy painting yet so diffident about how people might respond. Every day I'm wanting to plead with her to stop and yet wanting to admire the store of unexpected ideas in her mind.

It seems forever until she's finished. I've been grumbling for days about the height of the front lawn. It's a Saturday when she brings me out, down the path, and turns me. "The Great Kiwi Story," she says, modestly waving an arm.
I have to walk along it to take it all in, then stand out on the grass verge to study the whole then go across the road to make sure I've got the shape of it in my head. It's like a huge twisting snake or dragon. It's a montage of moments, all our heritages mingled together. A woman in old Chinese peasant garb with pants rolled up is pulling sea eggs from

under a rock ledge - so that's the *kina* taken care of - a tall Tahitian canoe prow beside her. People in *piupiu* and blankets are heating metal in a sort of miniature furnace, nails in baskets on the floor, one of them's licking a blistered finger. A character dressed like the Artful Dodger but with a queue of hair is up to his knees in a brown paddy field, face wrinkled in distaste, while a mandarin stands close by with what could be tax coins heaped in a policeman's helmet. A Polynesian girl, blossom over an ear and in a sarong rides a penny-farthing, and children in all sorts of costumes or none at all are running, playing, diving, working.

And about them, in all possible colours and a few I've never seen before, frolic *taniwha* in the guise of huge lizards or floating logs with eyes and snouts, European and Chinese dragons, stags, wolves, lions, *kiore*, pigs, unicorns, griffins, phoenixes, *moa*, crows, falcons, frigate birds, Haast's eagles, tuatara, the *Endeavour* with James Cook and a Dervish figurehead on the bowsprit, a tiny streamer, old style racing yachts, dinghies, junks, dhows, Moriori rafts. And in the distance are atolls, volcanoes, glaciers, palms, flax bushes, reefs, lagoons, lakes of lotuses, streams of eels. And defining the edges, seamlessly one joining the next, are rafter designs, Celtic and Anglo-Saxon and Chinese scroll work, *tapa* patterns. I spot more and more and more eye-captivating, dazzling hotch-potch, criss-cross vignettes of a 19th century from Mae's inventive mind. And I slowly begin to pick out painting styles from Impressionism, pre-Raphelite, Blakean, naïve realism, *sumi-e* figures in a medley of carving styles yet each full of life, scenes as if from Chinese scrolls to fragments that seem to be etched or imaged on a plate camera.

I realise I'll have to come back again and again to study it, to see afresh the whole and the parts I've probably not noticed. I feel a bit like an infant attempting to fit together the endless bits and pieces that are our world. Mae is watching me both proudly and apprehensively. I run and hug her to me. "Magnificent!" It deserves no lesser word.

So I get the lawn cut straight away, and even trim the trees, so now everyone can get a clear look at our house. At Mei's masterpiece. Its not long before it attracts attention, even while I am still out their sweating with the loppers and secateurs. People passing by to the shops stop and talk. Cars slow down. By the mid afternoon I've stopped the gardening, but I stay out there, by the letterbox, giving what is now a little speech. "It's a story of New Zealand. And we live right inside our own Kiwi dream."

I wonder about the possibilities. Maybe some postcards, T-Shirts.

But I realise as twilight settles, Mae has been absent, she won't come out even just to smile at all those looking.

The next day though she's outside again. Not standing proudly next to it, not talking to people. No, she is working again on the mural, and the next day, and the next. "A man called out from the footpath," she said, "that I should have Jains." "Jane who?" "No, the Indian religion, Jains. He showed me pictures in a book, he had brought it over specially to show me. So I'm putting them in you see, here."

"Alright," I nodded. And the Jains were finished.

And then: "Did you know there were rats here two thousand years ago, they can't bring themselves, so …."

And every night she was on Google, looking up information, tracking down not just how something or someone looked so she could render it indelibly into her mighty all consuming mural, like some botanist pins down a dead insect, but she also wanted to know the hows and whys of it - how did it get here, why did it come. All for the sake of authenticity. All because people kept coming up and pointing out their little bit of New Zealand heritage wasn't there.

She was looking up Macedonia now.

"Greeks!" I said at her shoulder. "Mae, it's finished, you don't have to include something for every single person who has ever immigrated here. You can stop." I say it over and over in many ways. You can stop. But it never does.

Because they came, like pilgrims to this mystical mural, drawn, not just to look, to admire, but a rag tag bunch, bringing their petitions for inclusion - as if appealing to the high priestess of paint, as if gaining a place in the Great Kiwi Painting, more than any certificate of citizenship, than any stamp on a passport, would secure them their identity here in our land. A diaspora of the dispossessed, attracted here. They were obsessed, all of them, and they fed into Mae, and she fed off them, as if she were taping into this great Jungian shared consciousness of longing that had for so long lain beneath the surface of our everyday transactions.

So it goes on. Day after day. Her face begins to look pinched, her eyes haunted. Sleep is something we snatch at. I wake again and again to find Mae is not in the bed or the room but sketching on her block of white pages, face intent with anxiety, trying to fit an image somewhere. "Mae," I take her arm, draw her towards the bedroom, "sleep, it can wait." But me too, I am often up, spend hours pacing. My nights are segues of post-modern videos: the happenings of the day, worries about Mae mingling, miscegenating with her mural … or nightmarish versions of it. We exist night and day within an unrelentingly morphing mural.

I come home late from work's increasing hours, and every day I find Mae no longer has time from her research, her preparation drawings, her meticulous preparing of outlines and figures, her painting. She cannot do washing, cleaning, shopping, contacting my parents, phoning Hong Kong. The mural has stretched round the side of the house now. I virtually pull her down one day from her plank to stop her painting across the windows of the spare bedroom. I smell her paints, her cleaning turps even in my office, while interviewing clients, on the train. I've a constant cough no medication fixes.

"Mae," I appeal one Sunday. "We should go away, have a break, enjoy a holiday."

She doesn't look up from her sketch pad. "Soon," she mumbles, "soon. I will be finished soon."

But no, soon never arrives. She has immersed herself, become a slave to her own work, as if this painting is somehow as vital as life, as if she was weaving into it the spiritual essence of our world, that if she stopped the world would lose some essential aspect of reality, as if the souls of us all were captured here in some hieroglyphic book of the dead and the living held by some ancient priestess. By Mae.

I am out in the garden, pruning again, giving my spiel again, by rote, to some new person who has driven up to look. Like the giant carrot in Ohakune, that house with Paua all over it down south, our place has become a Kiwi tourist attraction. But the person creating it still doesn't feel Kiwi enough. Not paying enough attention, with my head screwed round catching a glimpse of her down the side of the house now, feverishly working away - people now don't just stop on the footpath and look, I encounter them at all times of the day, just wandering around the section to look at the ever sprawling mural - I nick my finger with the cutters. Blood oozes and as I shake my hand, a drop arcs off and plummets to the ground, soaking into a bare patch of dirt. I stare at it. My blood with all the heritage of my ancestors coursing their way in chromosomatic waka down the rivers of the arteries - Maori, English, Welsh, god knows what other rag tag of inheritance is in there - my blood is in the land, the land is in my blood and I am Kiwi. I look at Mae, and I just then, right then, understand. She will always see in herself rice fields, chopsticks, strange and alien cities overflowing.

And seized by an idea I drop my cutters right there and just in my old gardening clothes run down the street and to the corner green grocer. "Carrot," I almost yell out. He points to where they lie. "Are they local?" "Local?" "Grown here, not imported." "Who imports carrots, you crazy? You people, you crazy" "What do you mean you people -" feeling very sensitive, what does he mean? my tiny bit of Maori? "You 100 milers, all have to be local produce, I seen it on the TV, look around, its all local of course. You think I get onions from Aussie, potatoes from USA. Crazy."

I snatch up the carrots and race back home, into the kitchen, peel them, slice and trim them, julienne style, tip them onto a plate, a dollop of mayonnaise and rush outside to find her round a corner half way up some jerry rigged scaffold, painting some bush - looks like gorse - she's even covering off the pests we brought over, someone brought over, bound to be related somewhere. "Here," I pushed them at her. "Eat." She looked down, as always preoccupied. "Eat," I said more sternly and she paused to pluck up a carrot and crunch it. "There," I said. "You are a kiwi." She looked blankly at me. "This carrot, planted as a seed in the black earth of this land, moistened by the tears of Rangi, warmed by the rays of Ra. Every molecule in this is from this land, you eat this, every molecule in it is transformed into your cells, bone, sinew - every bit of your body is infused with this land. Your blood. Here-" I thrust my hand at her, the finger yet again pooling blood, rubbed raw again by my washing and peeling. "This makes you Kiwi Mae, this - the land is in you. You are in the land. This blood makes us both Kiwi. You and me and everyone who lives here. Blood is what binds us all." She stared at me. Stared at my finger. Then a smile crept over her face. "You are a genius," she said. And bent from her scaffold and kissed me. Then she selected a fine tipped paint brush from her satchel, dipped it lightly onto my finger, catching up a smear of my blood and whisked it onto her mural, adding it into the yellow of gorse flowers, giving them the faintest additional gleam as she whispered "blood to bind us all," and then turned back to look expectantly at me, at my finger, as I stood appalled, she awaiting more drops to be offered up in supplication to the apotheosis of Aotearoa.

IF YOU LIKED THIS ….

home is one of a three part series of short stories by Eternal Gadd

A collection of eleven short stories on lust, longing, love and loss by a master story teller from Aotearoa. Meet Frank, the would be Romeo, bumbling his way into a honey trap, teenage Tania caught up in something she doesn't know how to deal with, John giving lessons to his teacher and Gabrielle struggling to come to terms with who she is. All of them caught in the web of Desire.

Whanau - 'family' in Maori - is a collection of fourteen short stories about family, friends, fears and faith. Lovers, mothers, grandparents and friends all trying to build that single most important aspect of humanity - love and the bonds of connection that make a family. They struggle against the odds, against the attempts of others to stop them, and against their own frailties and inabilities. You cannot fail to be moved by these gritty, authentic stories.

A home is what everyone desires - a place to truly belong, to be yourself, a shelter from the world, a place of certainty. Here in this collection of fourteen short stories, find people (and one dog) struggling to carve out a place for themselves. Meet Tokerau torn between her family history and her modern reality, Hoani and Pati seeking out Jerusalem, Nanny Paora trying to preserve her slice of land from the clutches of the Government and Mae who needs to know if she can say her home is truly hers.

ABOUT THE AUTHOR

Hallard Press is a boutique publisher based in Aotearoa, New Zealand and this book is one of a triology of collected short stories produced under the author name Eternal Gadd which is actually a psuedoname representing works from three generations of Gadds - all of them called David.

DA Gadd

David wrote mainly about growing up in New Zealand in the early years of the 20th Century when the family lived on the rural outskirts of the Auckland province. He was one of 12 children in a madcap family. He lived with a father intent on pursuing money making schemes and dreams into which he dragged the whole family with very mixed results and a long suffering wife. The family, as if not large enough of itself, was always being further enlarged by dogs, horses and the odd characters they encountered. As an adult David served in the Pacific during World War II, where he sustained a lasting injury. He was a talented writer of music, an amateur historian, always enthusiastic to jump in a car and travel around our beautiful country and a loving father and grandfather.

David Bernard Gadd

The main author of these short stories is DB Gadd, known to all as Bernard Gadd. He was a prolific writer of short stories, novels, plays and poetry, an editor of anthologies and literary journals and a publisher. All this, remarkably, was in his spare time. His main focus was as a teacher, the head of English at a college where he engaged in pioneering work in the classroom - this was the genesis of his writing, when he realised there were few authors writing stories relevant to the real lives of his students, who were mainly Maori and Pasifika teenagers living in a low socio-economic area of Auckland. So he began to write stories himself, designed to encourage literacy amongst students left behind by mainstream education. He engaged them by reflecting the experiences of their own lives in contrast to the sanitised versions of family life they were fed by most media. It worked, he captured their imagination and showed them the power of reading. His commitment to multi-culturalism also saw him foster a new generation of talented emerging Maori and Pacific writers and poets. He founded Hallard Press.

DS Gadd

Although he made his living writing, he was only ever a dabbler in writing of any worth. Instead he mainly concentrated on continuing the dubious Gadd tradition of a having a mad family surrounded by even crazier animals - all the while living with a beautiful, talented and (of course) long suffering wife, two gorgeous children and a variety of dogs, cats, rodents and goats.

OTHER BOOKS YOU MIGHT LIKE

Laya

Kidnapped by fugitives, teenage girl Laya is forced to become an apprentice to the dreaded, aging magician Langi. Frightened, lonely and angry she gradually accepts her place amongst these people and in the end, utterly unexpected, the future of them all is dropped within her hands. Can she decide for the best? The novel is set four thousand years ago amongst the sea voyaging ancestors of the Polynesians of the Pacific Islands. Fast paced and authentic, the story grips you and takes you there on the great canoes that settled the vast Pacific.

The more poetry you read, the better you write

A collection of essays on why reading poetry is something everyone who writes should do - every student struggling with essays, every businessman writing reports, every would be novelist - because reading poetry can make you a better writer. It includes essays on the haiku, dispenses with the complaints of rule-makers who try to restrain the haiku in moribund ancient formulae and urges every poet to try haiku - delivering maximum effect with minimum waffle.

CONTACT THE PUBLISHER

Thank you for buying this Hallard Press book.
We welcome feedback . You can get in touch via:

hallardpress@gmail.com

or follow our updates on

facebook.com/HallardPress

BECOME A FAN

www.ingramcontent.com/pod-product-compliance
Ingram Content Group UK Ltd.
Pitfield, Milton Keynes, MK11 3LW, UK
UKHW020235250726
13967UKWH00001B/379